The Power to Succeed

Sr. Elizabeth Ngozi Okpalaenwe

Langaa Research & Publishing CIG
Mankon, Bamenda

Publisher:
Langaa RPCIG
Langaa Research & Publishing Common Initiative Group
P.O. Box 902 Mankon
Bamenda
North West Region
Cameroon
Langaagrp@gmail.com
www.langaa-rpcig.net

Distributed in and outside N. America by African Books Collective
orders@africanbookscollective.com
www.africanbookcollective.com

ISBN: 9956-579-46-7

Opening Poem

History lives on when the writers sleep
Story may look old and outdated
Satiable minds renew its vitality
The experiences of heroes never sleep

A grim of light shatters darkness within,
A little smile wipes away mirth and misery
Misery is created by greed and jealousy
But the power to overcome lies within.

History repeats itself again and again
A new insight is discovered at its every round
Wise ones learn the message found
While fools stir in wonder again and again

Rise, my friend, claim the power within you
The power there is to change your situation
Why wash hands with spittle inside an ocean
Awake from your slumber, see the light within you.

Acknowledgement

It has taken quite sometime for this work to come to its final stage. I am immensely grateful to God for His unfailing mercy and love that sustained me throughout the period of this work. I am highly indebted to the Missionary Sisters of Our Lady of the Holy Rosary for their invaluable assistance, encouragement and care that helped me in this work. I am sincerely grateful to Rev. Fr. William Neba, who appreciated and edited this work, for his time, ideas and useful advice throughout the period of writing this novel. My profound gratitude also goes to Mr. Cyprian Diyen who read this work and made some corrections and strongly encouraged me to publish it. My gratitude also goes to Mr Peter Nsanda Eba, Rev. Fr. Englbert Kofon, Rev. Fr. Conrad Mhepo, Br. Francis Verye, Mr. Felix Awah Suh, and many others for their invaluable assistance throughout the period of writing this novel. I am indebted to my lecturer in Abia State University, Mr. C. Utenta, who helped me to develop interest in writing and the appreciation of values. I am also indebted to my family especially my brothers and my mother, who always support me with love and care. May almighty God reward each and every one of them.

Foreword

The well known saying "From grass to grace" always seems to describe the endeavours of super heroes. But here in this simple story the determination of a young lowly girl is rewarded with what human efforts are usually all about.

Mercy faces a lot of strain and frustration in her underprivileged life. She fights hard and overcomes many trials and deceptions with her mind set for the ultimate. Her self-mastery is very admirable. In the end she achieves her goals.

There is a very clear message that Sr. Ngozi has for the young, especially the girls who need to come out of ignorance. The fairly happy-ever-after part of the story makes for compelling reading, and the reality of the event situates well in our society.

I would wish every young and underprivileged person to have the courage and determination to be like Mercy.

Mr. Cyprian Diyen
OLLSS Mankon

Introduction

Have you ever been face to face with poverty? I mean the real poverty that never blinks its eyelids till it victimizes its prey; that makes one do anything just to survive? This type of depressing poverty needs a strong heart and a determined mind to resist its wanton worries and temptations that present themselves as the almighty god. It takes out one's breath to raise one's head high for a respectable position. Could poverty raise its head from grass to grace, from the downtrodden to the honest height? Could one who was actually poor from birth change the nature of one's background? This story tells us that it is possible. The will to change is all you need.

This is a fascinating story of a young girl from a very poor family who raised her head high and raised the dignity of women through her own personal and determined effort. She did not yield to the victimizations of corrupt minds, nor to the temptations of apathy and pessimistic thinking; rather she saw everything optimistically and through many hardships achieved her life's ambitions.

This story exposes the ills in our society. Some men and women have reduced themselves to fourth and fifth class citizens, living a debased life that deadens the conscience. Many healthy people shamelessly turn to the streets and want to snatch from the hard earned sweat of other people. We need open hearts and minds to effect a change that will benefit all. God always helps the poor who are honestly struggling. There is no easy way in life but life is easy when you accept your situation and make the best out of it. The happiest people are the honest struggling poor who believe that nobody has power over their life except God. You have the power and the right to choose what you want. Never sell!

Chapter One

Sleep left me in the middle of the night. I did not know what hour it was. It was something of an oddity. I felt a cold object lying beside me. What could it be? I remembered that my younger sister, Nelly, was sharing the torn mat with me. I, half- awoke, touched her placid body. She was drenched like a fish out of the deep. I half- stood, bewildered at the sound of the heavy down pour coming from the roof. In the urgent circumstance, I gently pushed my sister out of the pool, which had taken possession of our sleeping mat. She was deeply asleep and her sound, peaceful sleep greeted my effort to move her.

It was raining heavily and windy too. I got up, stood at the door, looking into the dark night. The trees slammed to and fro. The heavy rain often began with thunder and scattered wind. That night, the heavens seemed to be tired of its countless shootings and resigned to dripping like beads in self-abandonment. I was often fraught with fear when it rained because our house was often jostled by the wind, threatening to pull it down.

I tiptoed into my parent's room and saw a figure carrying our boxes and the utensils away from the run of the water which had gained entrance through the leaking roof and through the holes made by the reptiles and ants scrambling for shelter and food. I recognized her steps even in the dark. She carried our empty pot for soup and put it on top of a chair. A frog moved out of her way as she kicked her way through the dark. I guessed that her intuition would lead her to our room and so I tried to lessen her sorrow by tracing my steps back to our mat and lay in the pool of water beside my sister. I was shivering with cold like a small chick beaten by the rain, but I tried to be calm as my mother found her way to our room.

"My children were not disturbed from sleep," she murmured! She stooped down and touched my cold body.

She pulled us out of the water and got a piece of flat plank on which she made us lie on it. My sister coughed and I pretended to be fast asleep. My mother stood, looked sad and shed tears. She had known what it meant to be poor. I wondered what she was thinking as she stood looking at us. Was she recounting her life story or just feeling motherly for her suffering children? When I heard the sound of footsteps, I knew then that she was going back to her room. Would she sleep again? I doubted it. I was concerned to know what she would do next. I tiptoed to her door again. She was sitting on the edge of the bed, crying. Suffering had given her insomnia. Moved by her pitiful sight, I went back to our mat, lay down, covered my face with my hands and sobbed. I did not know when sleep overcame me.

Then I found myself in a big office. Curtains were hung on each of the windows and on the door. The room was equipped with an air-conditioner. At the centre of the room lay a beautiful rug and on it stood a desk framed with flowery formica with piles of books arranged orderly on top of it together with all writing materials. On the right of the room there was a refrigerator packed full with assorted drinks. I looked energetic and competent. I was the head of the institution. I sat on the chair, pressed a button beside the table and a girl came in. I gave her a message, which I cannot not recall, but she answered, "Yes madam." I answered many phone calls. Proudly as I was about to go for lunch, I felt a tap on my shoulder which woke me up. Oh! It was all a dream.

I woke up with a start. It was a Saturday morning, the end of July in the heart of the rainy season. My father, a heavy-jowled man, had been reduced to a sorry tale by poverty. I could describe him as a hardworking, loving and caring man. He had recently developed an uncaring attitude towards us. I think his poor condition contributed to his indifferent and selfish attitude at times. Musing over the past, I saw my father as a loving and industrious man who always

2

bought bread on his way back from the factory where he had worked as a cleaner. My brother, James, and I would sing with our shrill but gentle voices: 'Papa welcome,' when we saw the bread. He would carry us high in turns and make us laugh. He always looked for us whenever he came back and did not see us. Now poverty had made him become carefree. My busy mother, who, once upon a time was buxom, had been reduced to a slim, tall woman with an oval-shaped face, which gave her a childlike look.

My younger sister, Nelly, I believe, was ignorant of the extent of our poverty and of what happened last night. When she woke up in the morning, she was annoyed, supposing I was the one who bathed her with urine at night. She never heard the sound of the rain nor felt all the gentle pushes. I laughed while explaining to her all that happened.

Our parents had gone to the farm. I usually went with them, but this day I stayed back to tidy up the house. I was busy cleaning and emptying the containers my mother used to arrest the flood. Nelly went to the back of the house where she was cracking and eating palm kernels. It had become a routine in our house that breakfast was not considered; rather we made do with nuts or went with on empty stomachs till noon. My stomach ached and I begged her to remember my empty stomach since I was busy. I had scarcely finished when a sharp sound drowned my voice. Something had fallen. I ran in the direction of the sound and there was Nelly lying face downward. I shouted, ran to her, dragged her up. Encouraged by her breathing, I carried her along avoiding the stones though her legs were dragging behind on the rough surface. When I finally reached our front door, her dress was shredded and dirty. I ran inside, got some water and poured it on her. I was half relieved when she started crying.

What happened was that since it was a windy morning, the branch of a tree came down like a flash on top of Nelly. She could not avoid it. I was worried about her and wondered what to do but after sometime she slept and I

3

continued my cleaning. My mind wandered to the farm where my parents were working with empty stomachs. I could see my mother drinking from the small stream across the farm. My consolation rested on the fact that my mother would come home with something to eat. They came back late that evening bringing some tubers of cassava, vegetables, and some yams. I went straight to prepare the meal, our first and last for the day.

It was threatening to rain again. The night seemed to be filled with gloom. The nauseating situation of our hut had often put fear in the whole family. Night rainfalls always brought our poor situation to mind. I wished and longed for the dry season when we would sleep soundly without the molestation of the rain and thunder. Looking out from the kitchen, which was separate from our sleeping hut, I was enthralled by the number of lizards racing to join their normal line of action. Our hut was shared with these reptiles, which took possession of the roof and walls. They were not perturbed by our presence. The house was indeed in a poor shape and the roof was over-due replacement. Nobody cared about that since we hardly ever had enough to eat. Many nights we went to bed without eating anything.

When the food was ready, I shared it. Nelly could not eat well because of the pain from the accident. Our mother rubbed her with some balm which helped her to sleep. Of course, that was the only medicine in the house. Often she used it for all kinds of pains and sicknesses believing that menthol could cure all ailments. Once she had a very severe headache and she kept rubbing her face with menthol till a neighbour told her that she could use some natural herbs as a cure. This is prepared by boiling together the fresh leaves of mangoes, paw-paw, lemon grass, the peelings of oranges and stool wood. The vapour is inhaled and the liquid is drunk when it is cool. She used the herbs and indeed they were helpful. This then became our drug for treating malaria.

The village had no hospital. The only existing hospital was far removed from our village. It was a community hospital built by the local government. A doctor used to come from the main town once a month to treat serious cases. The hospital actually served only the rich since they were the only ones who could pay their bills. The poor had no place there and whenever the nurses noticed that you were poor, they treated you with contempt. I had never gone there but people told many stories of how people died there due to lack of drugs or through sheer neglect.

There was a sad story of a young boy who had died from snakebite. He had been taken to this hospital immediately after the incident. They had the anti-venom but when the nurse was about to load it into the syringe, the ampoule fell and the contents were spilled on the ground. Unfortunately, there was no other ampoule left. The boy degenerated and finally passed away. Some people said that the boy was just unlucky whilst others said that it was due to the carelessness of the nurse. Such incidents often put fear into people. The doctors and the nurses in turn complained that the government did not provide enough drugs in the hospital. Another side of the story was that the doctors and nurses used to cart off the drugs from the hospital to their private clinics and homes and then sell to patients. No one knows which is the true story.

Chapter Two

It was a moody day, cold and full of uncertainty. The sun had risen. It came half-full and wore a pale look like one who had lost the only son. The trees were as still as death. Suddenly, a gentle breeze started whirling, coming as if to give life to the sun. It stood alive as a slide-like colossus. The trees swayed to the rhythm of the breeze.

Looking out through the main door, I saw a woman coming towards our house. I recognized her as one of the wealthy spinsters who lived in the city. She was a middle-aged woman, tall and buxom. Her hair was woven and packed to the back, which gave her the look of the rich. She was not attractive though but she dressed expensively. I was scared at her broad face and wide brown eyes. She drew nearer and inquired about my father. Something like a spark pierced into my heart. I wondered whether her visit had anything to do with me. I had also heard rumours that she owned a hotel in Lagos and stories had been told how serviceable and available she was to her customers, but I did not really know what it all meant. I had no desire to ask either. I preferred to think about school and a government job and how I would one day put on high-heeled shoes and wear a long skirt like other girls.

Musing over the past, the picture vividly flashed in my mind how Patience and I used to wear high-heeled shoes made from empty tins of milk with an opening at the centre to hold the thread. We used to imitate the town ladies. Patience and I were from different villages but we were friends. I remembered the day we went to work in my father's farm. We used to share the days we worked in our fathers' farms together. That day, it was my turn. We left very early in the morning wearing our high-heeled tin shoes. The farm was far. The rain started drizzling by the time we reached the farm. It soon became heavy and made us cold. Since we could not work inside such rain, we ate the food we had and made for home. On our way back, Patience tripped on a stone, fell off her high-heeled shoes and started crying. It then dawned on us that we could not feign town ladies. We had to work and get money to buy real shoes. Later on Patience went to Lagos. When she came back a few years later, she looked like a real 'town lady' and I envied her. Then I learnt that she never went to school. I wondered what she knew about learning and fashion. On my part, I longed to move out of my environment and experience life elsewhere.

I was entrapped in my confusion when I heard my name. That woman smiled kindly and pitifully at me. 'You are going to live with Madame Ibe,' my father started; 'she has promised to send you to school as far as to the secondary level. This would give you a chance to enter into another world of life. You will become a real lady. Your mother and I did not go to school. That does not mean that we do not know the value of education.'

I was surprised to hear that and tears streamed down my cheeks. My father understood the meaning of my tears. My mother burst out and also started crying shrieking insistently

"No, John, you must be joking! You cannot send my daughter away too." She then narrated the trouble she had gone through because of James and his long absence from home. She ended in a sorrowful manner and my father begged her to sit beside him.

"This is a situation of a real need," my father explained.

"Madame Ibe has offered to educate her in school. The difficult times in our home have made me to look hopefully at her future. The future will be bright if she is educated. I know we need her in the family but the saying that 'a great traveller is wiser than grey hair' still holds good for me."

My mother started sobbing. I was sad to see my mother crying because of me. She, who was strong and courageous, was overcome by feeling. Madame Ibe was asked

8

to come back in two weeks time so as to give the family time to decide. She turned, smiled at me and left. I was awed by her smile.

At night I suffered from sleeplessness. Was that smile a sisterly one or one fraught with warning and danger? My spirits fell, all enthusiasm disappeared, replaced by indifference to the decision of my parents. I wondered what secret the future held for me! My parents discussed the issue of my going to Lagos later and agreed that I should go. I knew it was all my father's decision. My mother, however, would not want to stand on my way to progress though she was not happy. I had a feeling of awe as I went to tell our neighbours about my departure. There was an indescribable inner confusion mixed with hope. Nelly cried bitterly and wanted to follow me.

"Oh! stay, I will come back," I consoled her.

I gave her some of my old dresses, nursing the hope that I would get new ones in Lagos. My feeling found its expression in tears.

On the morning we were to travel, Madame Ibe came in a taxi to our compound. I felt like a little queen. I quickly picked my few belongings and off we went. The taxi dropped us at the park and we joined other passengers in a long big bus. We travelled along the long tarred road that leads into the big city of Lagos. The big modern mansions and large stores fascinated me. My eyes caught the mileage, which read **Lagos - 56kms**. That was all I remembered before sleep snatched my memory away. I was startled by the loud noise and shouts that bombarded my ears. I inquired from Madame Ibe what was wrong. She was busy bargaining with the bus driver on the amount charged for our load, though I had only a little bag.

The family I came to live with was a complicated one and I had to make myself part of it. Madame Ibe had three unmarried daughters. The first two had babies already. I wondered how Madame Ibe, who looked such a great disciplinarian to me, could have allowed that in her house. That was culturally unacceptable in my village for a girl to have a child when she was still in the father's house. In fact it was a taboo.

And in the Church, the parents of such girls were not allowed to receive Holy Communion. This was because we believed that every Christian family should teach and inculcate in their children, especially the girls, Christian morality and the acceptable behaviour in the society. Madame Ibe's youngest daughter was not far from my age, but she was already advanced in the way of the fashion of ladies. I learnt that she had refused to study because, for her, it was a waste of time. Her mother did not encourage her either. I had a different notion about life. The only thing which qualified one as a real lady, in my opinion, was education, that is, to know how to read and write.

I was shown into a dormitory-like room, which was shared by all the girls living and working for Madame Ibe. There were four beds. One was still vacant which was shown to me. I was awed by the magnificence of the room. It was too big in comparison to our two huts in the village. The dormitory served as a parlour as well as a sleeping room for us. I sat on the bed confused and dazed. One of the girls came to me and greeted me. She introduced herself as Charity though people called her 'Chay'. She proudly explained that she works in the hotel as a 'hostess' and when I inquired what 'hostess' meant, she laughed and told me not to worry and that I would soon know.

"Madame will introduce you muh! You look charming for our visitors," and then continued as if she was sent to direct me, "Em-m what is your name?" I told her, but when I was about to explain to her that I came to study, she left immediately as she heard madam's voice. I wondered what type of job a girl of her age and size would be doing in such a big hotel. Looking at her, she would be thirteen going to fourteen.

I was deep in thought when I heard madam calling. She began by telling me that I would have two days off to get myself acquainted with the place, and that Charity would show me round the premises where I would work and how to do it well.

"Work?" I stammered.

"I...I did not come to work madam, but to study and you told my father so."

"Listen," she retorted,

"I cannot send you to school when you have not worked for a year or two. If you perform well and satisfy our visitors, you will go to school."

She suddenly got annoyed for having to explain all this to me and shouted at me,

"No more two days off, start work tomorrow and you better comply with the visitors."

She banged the door and left. The phrase 'comply with the visitors' struck me like a sword in my heart just as the word 'hostess' kept me wondering what Charity was up to in that hotel. In my confusion I shed tears.

As I heard footsteps approaching, I quickly dried my eyes. Charity rushed in and asked me to follow her. I half got up and asked her where we were going to. She smiled and ordered me to follow her. She was going to show me round the hotel. I kept quiet and wanted to know what the job was all about. If it was housework like cooking and cleaning places, I knew how to do that well and that would not prevent me from going to school. We went out to the direction of the hotel instead. We went through the reception room, into the dining room, passed through the main hall into the restaurant and the kitchen. We came out on the pathway that leads to the laundry. The paths were demarcated with bougainvillea but they looked scanty and unkempt. Some abandoned hotel cars were parked here and there in a disorganized manner. We headed towards the rooms. Charity explained that some rooms were single while some double.

There were executive rooms for special clients. She explained that our job was to take care of these visitors, provide everything they needed and make them comfortable. If one performed her work well without any complaint from the visitors, madam would recommend her to the executive rooms. I struggled within myself whether to reveal to her my main reason for coming or to wait and see the nature of the work. She did not explain what we were to do for the visitors. I thanked her and followed her from one room to another.

When the showing was over, I sought the privacy of our room. When I reached there, to my horror a boy was lying drowsily on my bed. In anger I woke him up and asked him to leave. He got up half asleep, murmured something I did not hear and left. That night I could not sleep, as I was already home sick. The next day I went to work. I eavesdropped on the girls talking and sharing their experiences happily among themselves. One said that she was given "One T" (i.e. 1.000 Dollars) on the first day and madam gave her a tip. Another snobbed at her and said, "Muh! Only one T?" That she was given "1.5T" (i.e. 1.500 Dollars). Then another commented, "That new girl is beautiful, they will really enjoy her."

Then a car drove in and I heard Charity calling me, "Your visitor is here, comply and behave well. You know this is your first show," she said. Though confused, I ran in the direction of the car, took the man's bag and made for the room prepared for him. There was a pleasant ironical and amused smile on his face as he closely followed me. When I reached the door, I put the bag down to open the door. He tapped me playfully on my buttocks and said, "Still fresh." I was annoyed but I ignored him. Immediately I opened the door, with lightening speed he took the bag from me, dropped it on the floor and used his other hand to draw me very close to himself. I struggled. He was amazed and annoyed. In his masculine voice, he said angrily that I should behave. Before I could get my feet on the ground, he threw me onto the bed and fell on me. Instinctively I ceased to struggle and calmly told him to allow me to undress. He became happy and got up to undress himself too. I got up, went to the other side of the room pretending to undress. He finished, went to the bed and shouted, "Be fast girl." I was eyeing him carefully. In a flash I carried his bag and emptied the contents on his head, broke the glass on the table at his feet, threw his shoes on his naked stomach, opened the door and ran off like a deer. I ran straight into our room and locked the door.

It was then that I recalled what the man had shouted after me in his confusion, "Mad girl, catch her." He could not run after me since he was naked. It then dawned on me the type of work I was to be doing. The hidden meaning behind "comply with the visitors" and "hostess" became very clear to me. I concluded that I must find my way home. I could not do that dirty job. It was against God's commandment. My mother would frown at such an act. I was angry that Madame Ibe brought me out for prostitution. We were poor but we were morally sound. Besides, I was a Christian and a catholic for that matter. I knew that to fornicate is sinful. I made up my mind that I must go home. I could not do such a dehumanising job. We were poor, yes, but we had our dignity as a people of God. My mother's teaching and instructions came to my mind very strongly once more, "Mercy, my daughter, remember we are Christians. You are growing into a woman. Men will come to tell you how much they love you. Many of them are wolves coming to destroy you. Fornication is never allowed. Never sleep with any man until you get married. It is also in our culture that women should keep themselves pure until marriage. This will earn you a lot of respect from your would-be-husband and your parents will be proud of you. I will not be with you all the time. Therefore it is a life long struggle."

I never understood what she was saying at that time but now, yes. I was angry that Madame Ibe who came from the same cultural background like me should lure me into prostitution.

I had expected her to burst into the room, but it was Charity who opened the door and locked it behind her. "Why did you do that?" was the sharp question from her. I was very angry at that question and refused to answer to what I saw as ignorance about a woman's dignity by such lustful and immoral acts. "Well, I thought you knew," she went on, "that man was very scared."

"To hell with you and the man" I shouted. "I want to go home. Where is Madame Ibe?" Charity was taken aback at my outburst of anger and at my boldness to shout madam's name. "I wanted to study," I continued, "not to work in a hotel. I cannot act as a hostess, it is not for me."

"You will get used to it" she consoled. "Used to men's brutality," I shouted. "When you say this, you annoy madam," retorted Charity. I was furious at her defence of madam. "Get out!" I shouted at her. She left and I started crying.

Two days passed and everybody was still avoiding me. I could not locate madam's whereabouts. Charity stopped talking to me. I found refuge only in our room. On the third day, a man came looking for Charity. He looked at me, came nearer and said that I looked sick and added that I should take it easy. I thought to myself that they were all the same, but I needed to talk to someone, I needed help. Secretly, I felt like confiding in this stranger. I begged him to help me get out of the place. I told him my predicament. He sighed and sat down in a thoughtful mood. He told me that he would think about it. An intense dislike of the girls took hold of me. I found their views disgusting as a result of my Christian background and my conscience refused to concede. I was left in my own misunderstood world.

It was threatening to rain and my mind flashed back home, how the approach of the rain used to send a cold shiver through my body. I wiped the tears that had started rolling down like beads on my cheeks. I got out of the house and followed a strange road unaware of where it was leading me to. I marked the path with fresh green leaves to help me locate my way back. Hawkers were all around advertising their wares. With my heart in my mouth, I stood under an orange tree looking gapingly at nothing. Somebody coughed behind me and I turned sharply. The girl smiled. Looking at her, she looked young and intelligent. She had an oval face with a pointed nose, a small mouth and piercing eyes. I smiled back at her.

"My name is Felicia" she introduced herself. I kept smiling in spite of myself. "Where do you come from? You look sad" she continued. I told her where I came from.

She inquired again why I was standing there. I had no answer to give. I was afraid and not quite sure of what to say. We sat quietly for what seemed like ages. She must have sensed that I was becoming uncomfortable and so she started talking as if an inner power ordered her to do so. She told me that she had been lonely like me at one time when her own mother wanted to sell her off to marriage at the age of twelve but she refused. Everybody deserted her including her own brothers. It was odd and a very hard struggle. She ran away and slept in the bush for days. She could not go to her relatives because they were all in support of her mother. They also wanted a share of the dowry. One day, as luck would have it, a stranger offered to help her. She started hawking. He gave her a room to stay in. Then later on she was able to go to school.

I was fascinated by her story. She was a lucky girl indeed. She could educate herself with the gain she made from the sales. My hopes were raised, "but who would help me to begin?" I asked rhetorically. I told her my own pathetic story and my dream about going to school. She encouraged me to go and see her guardian. She advised me against going home to my parents immediately.

15

The air around me became relaxed and exciting. I nursed a new hope of surviving after all. How easy it had sounded. I stayed for three days with Felicia before I could see her guardian, Mr. Shilar. After narrating my story to him, he told me that he would investigate since he knew Madame Ibe. Two weeks later, Mr. Shilar called for me. He looked at me, breathed heavily and said that he met Madame Ibe who told him that I ran away a day after she brought me from the village. She lied that she had arranged for a place where I would attend an evening school until I was mature enough to go to secondary school. She told him many other things, which I could not understand. He advised me never to leave such a hard working woman unless I wanted to miss my chance in life. There was no opportunity to say a word and so I left dejected and disappointed. Outside, Felicia was waiting eager to hear the outcome of the discussion. I told her that I had been asked to go back to Madame Ibe, but that I must find my way home, back to my humble home.

It was a sunny day and the scorching heat from the sun was rather hurting. I found my way back to our room and sat on my bed. All the girls were at the work place. The room was quiet. I was a little confused on what to do next. Then the door opened sharply and there was Madame Ibe before me. I felt like digging a hole to hide myself. I lowered my eyes like a trapped rat. She laughed and sneered.

"So you took upon yourself to go out for exploration? You think I have time for such idiots like you. I brought you out from that swamp and filthy place you call your home to brush you up and all that you can offer is insult? You think you are more intelligent than the others? That man you ran to was a good man to have brought you back. You think life was so easy and yet your parents did not educate you? You want to go to school! Why didn't you think of school at your home? You are even privileged to have work, such a rare job."

Her voice changed and she was really raging,

"Now your naughty behaviour will earn you more filthy work than the one you have rejected. I don't even think men will accept to waste their energy on you again. You will work here for years without any pay. You might as well forget about going to school. You'll live here to rue your actions."

"No madam, please send me home. I want to go back home." I replied.

"Shut up" she shouted at me, slapped me three times and pushed me further away from her.

"You will die here. You thought you could insult my customer and go free?"

I ran to the door to escape not knowing that she had locked the door and put the key in her bag. She came where I was struggling at the door to run out, dragged me to herself, held my dress on the neck and tore it into two exposing my little breasts. I started crying. She held my breasts hard as if she wanted to pull them off and cursed, "An uncontrolled rag like you shouting at me! Whenever you will insult my guests again, I will pull these tiny things out of your body. Bastard."

I tried to cover myself but she roughly removed the remaining dress from my body leaving me stark naked before her. Her eyes seemed to be devouring my flesh. She then grabbed my breasts again and pulled hard until I screamed. She pushed me away and I lost control and fell. She looked wickedly at me, and told me to meet her at the laundry. She slammed the door behind her and left. Her slanderous utterances were rather hurting. I sat, cried and was really frustrated. I had made up my mind to go home and forget about my fantasy of school rather than facing that disgusting woman. I detested being a harlot. My whole strength and mind was geared towards home. I sat quietly to think after I had cried for some time. I did not have even a farthing to help me to go home. I decided to take the drastic action to go home and give up my ambition.

When the girls came back that night, it was Charity who came to ask me where I had been for the past weeks. I remained silent because I was not in the mood for discussion. I could not trust any of them. Throughout the night they were talking and giggling about what I do not know. They looked at me and laughed. I was very hungry but I could not ask for food since nobody cared. They displayed on the table their new shoes and other gifts they received. I was weak, tired and their debilitating chattering did no good to revitalise my condition. In silent tears and agony I slept.

Chapter Three

I was startled by a whisper. I thought it was in a dream. I opened my eyes, peered through the window and saw a figure staring at me. Fear gripped me. I was about to shout when I recognised who it was. It was the boy I confided in the day I wandered away from the house. He beckoned on me to come near to the window. With great circumspection, I got up and went near to the window.

"You have to work like a drudge to gain your freedom from Madame Ibe," he started immediately in a very low tone, and continued,

"I have an aunt who urgently needs a baby sitter."

He described her as a woman but who was hard to please but that she would pay me enough money to take me home. The place was far from Lagos and Madame Ibe would never find me out. He half stooped and looked at me and asked; "Do you want to go or not?"

The demands of the moment made me to abandon my fate to that stranger's new idea. I tiptoed back, collected my few belongings, unbolted the door gently and followed my fate.

An unexpected breeze dominated that time of the night. The trees swayed to the rhythm of the breeze as we passed groups of people loitering here and there, talking, smoking and laughing merrily. I could not recognise the road we took since it was pitch-dark. We must have walked for more than three hours, yet no one uttered a word to the other. I was tired and hungry, but I dared not complain. I was like a lamb being led to the slaughterhouse. We came out from a thick bush onto another untarred road. I prayed that we would see at least a building that would suggest some human habitation but none was in sight. Then I became really afraid and reprimanded myself for such a quick decision.

I was battling within when my companion suddenly stopped and said to me,

"We will stop here and wait for a taxi."

The night was long. I stayed by the side of the road with a total stranger till morning. We then travelled almost the whole day starved to death. I tried several times to inquire about him, but he only revealed his name as John, a relation of the woman I was to stay with. It was at nightfall when we finally reached the place. On our arrival, John ran into a building and came out as fast as lightening followed by a tall woman. The woman stood for what seemed like ages gazing at me. It looked as if she was counting every single bone in my body. I took the same opportunity to look at her. She was fair in complexion, slim with dry cheeks like a stockfish. She flashed a sharp look at me and asked what they called me. I did not hear her or rather I was afraid already. She shouted the question again and I was startled and answered,

"Mercy."

"From where?" came another question.

"From Ikem, Anambra State."

She then continued as if I was very far away from her as she questioned me on my experience about baby-sitting. I told her that I had never done that before but that I would do my best. She told me that she had three children I must take proper care of, with a long stress on the word "proper" and that I could not see them then since I came late, with great emphasis on the word "late." She then went on,

"I heard you worked in a hotel. I hope you have good manners. I will give you a trial anyway." She turned and started talking to John as if I was no longer there. When she finished, she turned and went into the house. John turned and smiled to me. He told me that that was the woman I would live with, that she could be tough but I needed a lot of patience. He reminded me that I needed to work and earn enough money to go home though I was not sure weather he told her that. Before John left, he promised to visit me in the nearest future.

When I turned I saw a girl waiting for me. Without greeting or any introduction she took my bag and I followed her silently. We passed one room after another till we reached the end of the long building and there was my room. It was very untidy and out of human touch. I got into cleaning it. Cleaning my room on my arrival would not have been a problem just that I had not eaten since the previous night. I was left with weary bones and tired limbs as I went to bed. I woke up the following morning with a start to find the door of the room where I had slept securely locked from the outside. I was surprised and wondered what gave rise to that action and what that could mean. My stomach ached and I wanted to ease myself too. I waited for what seemed ages before madam briskly opened the door and thundered,

"You dam fool, you were still sleeping. I hope you have not come here to dawdle away your time. How long would it take you to know that you have a duty to perform? Get up from there, go and meet the children."

That was how I was introduced to the children. I left immediately for the parlour and when they saw me they started giggling. By way of an introduction I called my name. The laughter grew louder. I was not sure what to do. I stood there like a fool while each one of them described how I looked like. Uncertain about how I should respond, I simply put on smile. Back in my mind, I wondered what I was expected to do but there was no other introduction to my duty. I picked up courage and called Paschal.

"Fool, he has gone to the school," came a voice from within.

I then presumed that Paul must have also gone, so I called Pauline the youngest one. She ran out towards me, threw her doll baby at me and said,

"You resemble that."

I laughed and playfully threw it back at her. Then we started playing.

"You are not a doll baby after all," she exclaimed.

"You can play and laugh. This doll baby cannot play and Raphaela does not play or laugh."

"Who is Raphaela?" I asked.

"She left this morning" she went on.

"I hated her because she did not play with me. She often beat me."

"No, you should not hate people" I retorted.

"Why not?" she insisted.

"It is not good and more so we are all God's children," I went on.

The words seemed to have taken hold of her, so she looked at me and said she was hungry.

It was through Pauline that I came to know that Raphaela was the girl who had shown me to the room previous night. She had lived with madam for four years and had been sent home without any preparation. I also learnt about some of the day-to-day activities from little Pauline.

Mrs. Patty, as she was called, was a businesswoman who had lost her husband four years ago shortly after the birth of Pauline. She used to get up very early in the morning, prepare meals for her children before going for her business which was not all that easy for her. When Raphaela came, she could not meet up to her expectations. She was a calm, quiet person, who Mrs. Patty saw as a lazy person. All her efforts to please Mrs. Patty only earned for her beatings and abuses which did not help the situation. The story of Raphaela injected fear in me and I decided that I would inquire from madam her expectations of me.

After feeding the children in the evening, I went to the parlour to see her.

"What is it Mercy?" she thundered as I opened the door.

I stammered out of fear and surprise at her loud voice.

"I......I just wanted to know your expectations of me in my job."

22

She got up, gave me a good slap and said,

"Day in day out you do not know your job. You will receive a slap or two like this everyday and then you will know. I have three children to bring up and I do not need another burden."

On reflection, I recalled how I used to wake up early to get things ready at home, but the problem was that I did not know what to get ready and the way to do it satisfactorily. I found myself at crossroads. I decided to do what I could and receive her thunderous corrections.

It was like hell one day when I got up early and prepared yam porridge for breakfast. Then I steeped the dirty clothes in a basin and since it was still dark, I decided to stay back in my room till such a time that I could sweep the rooms. To my horror, a loud knock got me onto my feet. On opening the door, I saw madam filled with rage. I could not escape.

"You again! Raphaela is gone and now is Mercy." She slapped me again and again. Indeed a strange fear overwhelmed me. The last words I heard before I lost consciousness were from an old woman who had just come in.

"That's enough. It's enough."

When I regained consciousness, I saw Pauline beside me ready to show me her doll baby to play with. I made every effort to play but to no avail since I was weak and in pains.

"Why was I beaten so mercilessly? And who was that old woman who came to my rescue?" I inquired from Pauline.

"I don't know," she answered. Then she went on, "Mummy said that you prepared yam poo. And I do not eat yam poo in the morning." "Waste, waste" she said.

Back in the kitchen the food I prepared was left untouched.

"What did you eat this morning?" I asked Pauline.

She listed them, "Tea, bread, an egg, cornflakes and Quaker oats."

"Do you eat all these everyday?" I went on.

"No," she answered.

"What type of food do you eat in the afternoons?" I continued. Then she said,

"Rice, Yam foo-foo and couscous."

Then rhetorically I asked,

"But how would I know which to prepare?" To this question she had no answer.

I ate a bit of the yam and gave some to Pauline in the afternoon.

When she slept, I decided to leave the house for a while. I climbed the hill at the back of the house. Then I saw dwarf hills which surrounded the house in an oval shape. It was naturally decked with scattered dwarf trees bearing flowers of various scented colours. It gave a beautiful scenery from the slope. It was like the angels' garden sloping from the top down in a chisel like manner. Inspired by the tranquillity of the place, I busied my mind with the situation I found in my new home. There was no solution on the sorrowful condition of my life yet I did not want to go home empty handed.

I very soon sensed that I was not alone as I felt a shadow behind me. I could not turn to look. Fear gripped me. The breeze seemed to echo my name. As a child I was told never to answer a call when I was not sure of the caller, for, it could be an evil spirit calling to take my spirit away. It was a superstitious belief though. The voice became clearer and clearer and I was scared when I saw an old woman coming towards me.

"Who is she?" I wondered.

I was on the verge of running off when she called again and assured me not to run. She came out mainly to talk to me. She was one of our neighbours. She was the same woman who had intervened on the day I cooked the yam porridge and I had been badly beaten. Her hair glittered like silver. Her teeth were fastened in her jaws as she spoke. That gave her the look of one who had seen many difficult years. Her eyes like diamond made her look like a rat gazing out of the hole. Her presence made me a little bit uncomfortable. When she spoke, her voice was counter-tenor and encouraging. I stood there struggling to keep a straight face. When she inquired about my home, I instinctively felt I could confide in her. So I told her my story and ambition in life. In between my story, the tears from my eyes also told their own story. A glimmer of hope also flashed in that exercise. It was not a great hope of expectation from her but for the fact that someone was interested in my life.

"My child," she started, "Your story is the familiar story of the great heroes in the world. In spite of our frustrations and nasty experiences, we must continue to strive to achieve what was destined for us. Our aim must be brought to fruition. Force landing requires tactful persuasion. You have to play the fool very often to wear the crown. Everyone possesses a hidden softness unbroken. Let your honest service break your madam's hidden tenderness. No matter what happens, you must try to see her as your mother. You have an aim and a goal."

When she finished and turned to go, I thanked her and returned to the house feeling better. It was a chance meeting. I believed it was destined to happen that way so as to revive my drooping spirit to a hopeful future.

On my return, I found my door locked with a new key. I held my breath. There was a dour silence everywhere. Pauline had woken up from sleep and was playing with her doll. Madam had returned and was in the parlour watching a program on the television. I greeted her but there was no answer. In my confusion, I was in a dire need of help. Madam's reticence was often more mysterious than revealing. I cooked the evening meal, fed the children and summoned the courage to go again to her. I stood there unnoticed, unrecognised like a rag. Her attention was fixed on the exciting movie on the television. I must have stood there for more than two hours when she got up, put off the television and went to bed. The children had already gone to bed. I decided to sleep in the parlour but she came out after a quarter of an hour and drove me out of the house, put out the lights and locked the door. I slept outside in the cold without even a wrapper to cover myself.

I inquired from Pauline the next day why her mother locked my door. She said that it was because I left the house while she was away and that she has found me "a hard - hearted person who has refused to cry when I am wrong." I wondered what that could mean. Pauline explained that Raphaela, the girl who left a day after I came, used to cry and madam used to beat her a lot and in between the beating, she would learn what she had done wrong. That was a terrible way to learn I said to my self. How could I cry without any reason for it! Moving to the back of the house was not a crime for me. As to crying, that sounded very ridiculous. Raphaela was sent away despite her efforts to comply with all that madam wanted. I must not show such weakness but I promised to do my best. I became aloof with the situation and refused to allude to the un-communicated treats of madam. In spite of the cold and chilly air outside, I slept behind my room for days, picking and eating whatever I could lay hands on since she stopped me from entering the kitchen. When I could no longer tolerate the neglect, the maltreatment and the silence, I ran to madam when she was entering the kitchen and pleaded, "I am really sorry for what I did wrong, please forgive me."

She looked down at me and half shouted, "I do not want to touch you Mercy, because if I do, you will die, and I will not even know the bush or forest to carry you to."

She shuffled her dress as she paved her way through the door and left me looking confused. Then suddenly she turned back and shouted at me, "Away with your shaggy eyebrows and shabby clothes. I find your character disgustful and I detest your bad manners. You need many months of serious training on how to live in a place like this. Maybe it is too modern for you having come from the village. I have told you time and again that I do not want an additional burden or else I will send you packing."

I bowed my head as if adoring her every nasty word. When she finished, she threw the key of my door at my feet. I picked it up and walked away feeling really like a slave.

"Why am I so unfortunate in life?" I wondered.

My own mother would never treat any child like that whether the child belonged to her or not, because she believed that all children came from God. The more I tried to accept Mrs. Patty as my mother, the more she ignored me. What mattered was her own children and herself. I wondered if there was any softness of heart in that woman as the old neighbour had told me. Maybe the soft heart was reserved for her children only. How could I penetrate that soft place? Will love and patience change her as I hear the priests preach in the Church? Had I enough love and patience to endure all these and for how long?

Chapter Four

It was windy. The trees around swayed in the strong wind, which signalled that rain was at the corner. I could hardly stand to enjoy the breeze, for, behind the lines of the coconut trees which were swaying to and fro in the wind, I saw what looked like a human face coming in haste towards me. Somewhat frightened, I was about racing away when I heard my name. I recognized the voice immediately and behold it was John, the man who had brought me to Mrs. Patty. John came with some news and a letter from home. I was excited to know how he got my letter from home. Who could have written the letter? My parents were illiterate. Then a sudden fear gripped me. John held the letter tight while he told me other stories. He narrated what happened after my disappearance.

Initially, Madame Ibe took it with a pinch of salt and swore that she would bury me alive whenever I came back. She was so sure that I would return but as the months rolled by, she became worried and started interviewing the other girls. Charity suffered most because she was thought to be closest to me. The girls were taken to the police station, interrogated and tortured for a couple of days in a bid to get information from them. There was no news about finding a missing girl anywhere either. Madame Ibe went home, returned with a letter but dropped it carelessly in the girls' room. When she could not find the letter the next day, that became another point of suspicion. John had secretly taken the letter to bring to me. Madam then suspected that one of the girls must have planned that with me. Charity confided in John, her friend, and he advised her to take it easy. My mother wrote the letter and in the language I would understand.

"*My child Masi,*" as she normally called me. "*Madame Ibe told us that you have started school and you are doing fine. Thank God. We, too, at home are fine. James came home for a little break and longs to see you. He is very tall and fat now. Your father had asked Madame Ibe to allow you to come home for Christmas. Your friend Patience is back at home, too. I gave Madam the new dresses and shoes James bought for you. Your mum."*

And at the corner of the paper, Nelly scribbled her own lines; *"Mey! I miss you. I cannot understand the type of strange questions your Madam asked our parents about you. I hope you are fine as she told us. James said I shall soon start school. More stories for you at Christmas when you come back. It's me Nelly."*

I was sad and heart-broken after reading the letter. I ran to my room and John followed to know the contents of the letter. He could not bring the dresses and shoes because madam did not leave them where he could find them. How could she tell such blatant lies to my parents? I held back my tears to tell him what was in the letter. Many ideas came clustering in my mind whether to find a way back home or to go back to Madame Ibe and demand that she should fulfil her promise. She was really a dubious woman.

"You will do neither of them Mercy" intercepted John.

"Rather you will start school here. Write and tell your parents where you are and caution them not to tell Madame Ibe."

"No. My parents will not keep it to themselves. I want that Ibe of a Madame to tackle the mystery on her own life and have the chance to tell more lies till the bench is filled with her lies."

On the one hand, I was longing to go home but education stood on my way bestriding the narrow and dangerous way. I must not close the door to my future too quickly. John inquired about my life with his aunt and I narrated to him how it had been. I told him how much I had earned. I never bought any new dresses or shoes since I came. I still had the worn out old dresses Madam gave me last Christmas. I told John that I would like to begin school as soon as possible. He promised to speak to Mrs. Patty about that. At night I prayed in silent tears to God to help me and to change Mrs. Patty's heart.

In the morning, I went about my duties. I was worried and anxious. Anxiety crept in as the urge to go home increased, but I felt it was a passing emotion that would vanish soon. The exuberant urge for knowledge surpassed other feelings. John encouraged me to keep saving my allowance and not to lose hope. He also advised me to leave Madame Ibe to sort out the mystery of my disappearance. He stayed for two days and went back to Lagos.

It was a debilitating atmosphere. The sun had risen earlier than usual. The sun is a wonderful creation of God and its face usually has its own hidden message. The house was empty since the children had all gone to the school. I locked everywhere and went out through the back door. I had never gone beyond the small hills behind the house. Madam had warned me several times not to leave the house or welcome any visitor especially when she was away. I did not understand the reasons behind those instructions though. My intuition kept urging me on to discover my surroundings. The thought of facing madam's brutal and insulting corrections deterred me. I felt too that I needed to explore my surroundings in case of any unforeseen circumstances.

I began to wander along a winding path till I burst into an open square. The set-up was like a village square. Woods polished in red and white were placed at the centre in a sitting position. The environment was clean and inviting. I passed through and went in the direction of the market. I looked to the right and I saw what looked like a school building. It was long and had five doors. There was a board at the gate with a writing that I could not read.

I stood there gaping at the letters as if they would reveal a secret to me. It was not a market day. I was so happy to see a school building. I heard voices coming from there but there was no one in view. I stood contemplating whether to go further or to return home. I would not like madam to

31

come home before me. Then I felt a hand on my shoulder. Before I could turn, two hands went to my eyes and covered them. I could hardly guess who it was because I had no friends and not to talk of knowing anyone in that strange place. I knew that whoever it was must have erroneously taken me for a friend. The hands lingered on my eyes too long for my liking. When I struggled to remove them, they moved down to my breasts. Then it dawned on me that there was danger. I turned sharply and pushed the boy away. We struggled till he saw he could not over power me and said among other things in broken English, "You are not in school, nor in the market nor at home, what then are you looking for at this ungodly hour?" I was tongue-tied. He started coming towards me again. Then I saw two other boys coming behind him. I took to my heels and the boys ran after me. I raced off in full speed, entered the gate and locked it. They stood at the gate hurled abuses at me and cursed themselves for not being fast enough to get me. Could it be that bad boys were moving about when others were busy? I wondered. I decided to find out from Paul when he came back. The next day, I called Paul outside the room and asked why do people not move about at any time especially in the afternoons? He had no answer to give, but just said that mummy did not want that people should be lazy and that evil spirits move about in the afternoon and swallow children who do not want to be obedient to their parents.

After that incident, we had a visitor. I went and prepared a room for him. The idea of preparing a room for any visitor reminded me about my stay with Madame Ibe. When I had finished, I went and carried his bag. The bag looked familiar and I remembered that I had seen that bag somewhere. Fear gripped me as I recognized the face of our visitor. Could he be a brother to Mrs. Patty? The children called him uncle Joe. He was the same man I threw the bag at in Madame Ibe's hotel. It was the same bag he carried at that time. I lowered my eyes praying that he should not recognize

32

me. I feared that Mrs. Patty might tell him my story which might re-waken his memory. I became anxious and prayed that my sudden nervousness would not reveal my identity. I was worried and eavesdropped at every conversation.

I showed him to his room. As I turned to go, he called me to wait. He made as if he had something to say but decided against it. I stood and observed him with care. I felt he was struggling to say something. He looked like a dubious man who loved to exploit little girls. Such people never like to get married. I wondered how he could be a brother to Mrs. Patty who was very strict and hard to please. I remembered the day she told me how and why she sent away Raphaela and warned me sternly never to talk to any man. When Uncle Joe finished devouring me with his eyes, he recollected himself and asked where Raphaela was. I told him that she had been sent away. He was disappointed. He asked if I could come and help him wash his things. I told him that he had to tell madam before I could do it. He was not happy with that answer but said nothing. I left feeling happy that he did not recognize me. A day before he left, I overheard him arguing with madam about something which I could not tell. He left after three days. I was relieved. After that visit, I made a decision to explore my surroundings further in order to understand the dangers around me. It was better to know the dangers than to be ignorant of them.

The day was dull and gloomy or rather I felt gloomy. Two weeks had elapsed since Uncle Joe's visit. The sun was hot and hurting. I found it uncomfortable to stay in the house since I detested the restriction placed on my movements. I opened the gate and stood looking into the thin air. I was deep in thought when I felt a shadow behind me. Turning sharply I saw a strange face. There was confusion of feelings whether to shout, run or stand.

"Who are you?" I half shouted in fear. The man laughed in a funny manner and said, "I saw you when one of my friends was harassing you at the square. I thought you

33

were Raphaela. I am a great friend of Raphaela…" Then he continued, "You look worried and frightened, just like Raphaela."

I had time to observe him as he was talking. He was of short of stature with a round and plump face. He wore an expensive pair of black trousers with a light blue shirt. He wore some dark goggles, which made him look wayward but affable. But when he laughed, he did it in an ostentatious manner. I became indignant and ordered him to deliver his message and leave me.

"I just wanted to see Raphaela," he said quietly.

I told him that Raphaela had gone. I was spared further questions by the appearance of Pauline. Unfortunately, madam was with her. She saw the boy and I knew that to defend my innocence about his visit would be like pouring water into a basket. Madam never asked me any questions but went into action according to her own judgement. Actually I knew this would come. She called me into the room and without further delay beat and kicked me mercilessly.

"Idiot, you should have remained in that hotel. This is not a place for prostitutes. You will soon be pregnant like Raphaela. I will kill you before it happens."

She tore my dress exposing my inner wears. Tears rolled down my cheeks like beads when she started cursing and abusing even my family. I felt humiliated. Then she suddenly stopped and left me there. I received the beating and insult with courage. I knew it was transferred aggression. It was then that I made up my mind to do something quickly before I was killed.

The dry season was at its peak and the sun was hot. The sweat from my body could form a small stream. My clothes were soaked in my sweat. I had finished the washing when madam called me. She had to travel to the village for three days for an urgent meeting. The instructions on how to behave and treat her children could not contain in any book.

Having mastered her ways like a poem, I simply listened without coughing.

The next day, I took the children to school for the first time. I felt it was an opportunity to discover places and plan my escape. I followed the left turn from the school gate and found myself inside the town. The magnificent buildings and the beautiful road construction entranced me. Some of the roads were tarred but narrow compared to the ones found in the big cities like Lagos. I wondered where the long road would lead to. I moved on and met a small girl from whom I inquired the name of the place. She spoke a strange language that left me puzzled till she walked out of sight. I passed many signboards but I could not read the writings on them since it was written in a local language. I guessed that I must have gone far, so I turned back hoping to ask Pauline about the place. After supper, I joined the children in the parlour. They were surprised to see me. Pauline was happy and showed me her work at school. I looked at the letters, which of course made no sense to me and praised her for the good work. The others became free with me. I learnt that the town I saw was called Quashi. The villagers owned it but it was given to migrants from Egypt who came to trade with the people there. It used to be called 'No Man's Land.'

I tactfully found out how many schools there were in the town and the conditions for accepting a foreigner. It was Paul who innocently told me that they would never admit me in any of the schools because of my ignorance of the native language and the funny way I spoke English. Besides, their mother had said that I could not go to school due to my inability to learn. She feared that if I learned the language, I would be anxious to start school and then the work at home would suffer or I may become pregnant like Raphaela. I hid my surprise at that discovery and diverted the topic to something different. I told them a lot of funny stories about animal behaviour, love and hate which made them to laugh and roll on the floor.

When I went to bed that night, I was disturbed and could not sleep. Would it not be better to go home and forget about education? I had sharp pains and headache trying to figure out what was the best thing to do. There was practically nobody to turn to for advice. I dare not risk writing to John in case it may fall into wrong hands. There was no friend to share my thoughts with.

The next day when the children had gone to school, I left the house again looking for a quiet place to sit and put my thoughts together. It was a devastating moment for me. I wandered absent-mindedly into the unknown. I did not know how far I had travelled away from the house. I was startled by the loud noise of children hunting in the bush. I became confused as the boys ran out of the bush in my direction. I saw the big rat they were chasing run past but I also took it that they were after me as well. So I ran off like a deer while they ignored me and continued chasing their game. I heaved a sigh of relief and went back to my thoughts.

Then I heard my name echoed in the wind. It sounded like the voice of my younger sister. Then I heard it again. It was a man's voice but familiar. The name became real in my ears.

"Who could know that name here?" I wondered.

I turned and behold there was a strange man standing next to me. He was tall and stout. He smiled calmly.

"You do not recognize me," he said, "but what brought you here Mercy" he inquired.

I was shocked at the mention of my name.

"Are you not Mercy from Ikem?" he asked.

"From Ikem" I repeated more confused. He smiled and said he was Jude, my elder brother's friend. I then saw the familiar face and screamed. I hugged him. Jude left for town at a very young age when I was only 5 years old. He was already twelve years old at that time. He was older than my brother but he loved him with all his heart.

"You have changed almost into a woman" observed Jude.

Then he inquired about home, which had become alien to me. I told him my story and my utmost ambition in life. I told him how I discovered Mrs. Patty's plan to keep me away from my dream. I ended up by saying that I longed to be free from her to begin school but it seemed impossible. Jude was stupefied by my story and offered to take me out of the place.

We went on to discuss the best way to leave Mrs. Patty without creating any scene. I told him that the money I had saved would help me to begin while doing some other work. To avoid any confrontation, I decided to leave the house before Mrs. Patty came back. I prepared the children and sent them to school with the hope that before they came back their mother would have come back too. It was on the day she was to return that I took my destiny in my hands to an unknown destination. I dropped a note thanking her for her care and love. I told her that I could not continue to live with her without any hope for my future. I asked her not to look for me because I have gone for good. I made sure that I locked everywhere and dropped the key of the gate right next to it. I knew that the children would come back first to discover the key. I felt like telling the old woman who advised me but I did not want any contrary opinions about my decision.

Chapter Five

It was cold and chilly. The weather seemed to be revolting with my plight. The little birds were in their own world hopping on the privet hedges. Their colours looked prismatic. The environment was strange and seemed to hold unfolded information. Jude's residence occupied a central place in that vicinity. I did not see him through out the morning. He lived alone in a big magnificent house and in a lonely place. I wondered why he had not married. I startled back into the present when Jude came into the room in the late afternoon. He planned to take me to Jos to stay with a friend of his for a short time while going to school.

It was a far journey into the unknown and that sounded adventurous too. But the fact that I was going to begin school made a lot of difference. I promised Jude that I would be of great help in domestic activities in his friend's house. I felt too that I should write home through Jude. I believed firmly in my fate. The money I had saved would keep me for at least two years. I hoped to find petty jobs here and there while studying. I wondered whether the new family would be good to me and in that great uncertainty, I set out for Jos with Jude, knowing fully well that I was alone but having a firm faith that out of darkness light would shine.

The family I was introduced to was Chike and his wife. I was welcomed to stay till I got another place. Jude pleaded on my behalf after narrating my story to them. It was a place he used to stay whenever he came to Jos.

Jude left the next day. I had wanted to write home through him but something prevented me from doing so. I wondered if Jude would go home and tell my parents where I was. I knew my mother would not believe the story unless she heard from me. She might get into a row with Madame Ibe who was still hiding my disappearance from them. I wondered what lies she had told them for the past four years and for how long she would continue. I had lost the only link

I had. I knew John would not forgive me for my actions. The urge to survive knows no bounds. One must lick ones tongue before the harmattan applies its unwanted charity.

One week after, Chike informed me that he had found a room for me somewhere in the town. I was surprised, for, I had expected to stay with them for a little bit longer period than that. In that case I thanked him and took my few belongings to my new home. The first thing I decided to do was to get something doing to earn some money. There was a woman, a baker, just opposite the place I was staying. I went and begged her to teach me how to bake with the offer to pay for the training. She accepted and we agreed on a schedule of two hours every afternoon, thus from 4.00 p.m. to 6.00 p.m. from Monday to Friday every week. I learnt how to bake a lot of things from her– cakes, chin-chin and doughnuts. This schedule gave me ample time to go to school in the morning and then work in the afternoon. Chike was very helpful in getting a school for me.

When I went to the school to register in Class One, the head teacher was surprised at my age and height. He queried why I never started school in time. Chike begged him to see how he could help. I answered all the questions he asked me. He then said that with my experience and intelligence he would get a private teacher to help me so that I would not go through all the classes. I worked tirelessly after school going through the class one books and notes and then doing the assignments given by the teacher and learning my trade. It was difficult. Apart from learning how to bake, I also engaged myself in another job. On Saturdays after washing my clothes, I would go to the nearby forest to fetch palm fronds. These I cleaned into nice brooms, divided them in bundles and sold to the teachers and students in school. Such brooms looked common but were scarce in that part of the country. The little money I got from the sales helped to keep my bag from being dry. I bought books and other things I needed and paid for my tuition at the bakery. I was self-reliant. Very soon I began to speak and write a little English. It was a great joy for me to speak and write in English.

I had a great urge to write home, then to John who must have heard what happened and then to Jude but I kept on delaying this. I tried to visit Chike and his family any time I had the chance for they were the only guardians I had. When I went to Chike's office to tell him about my progress in school, his wife complained that I did not visit them often. The simple reason was that I had a rather tight schedule most of the time. I actually went to the office that day because I wanted to share my worries about Jude with them. I felt that Chike, being an old friend of Jude, would know why Jude was living in such an isolated place. I told him how I knew Jude. Indeed he knew his story. It was a long story indeed.

Jude was an ambassador for his village when he got married. It happened that two years after his marriage, he was chosen to represent his village in a foreign land. It was all about the autonomy of his village from other neighbouring villages. A body was set up to look into the matter. A agreement in opinion could not be reached since Jude refused any bribe that would go against the freedom of his people. He was caught and locked up in prison together with others who refused the bribe. He was there for a year. One day, a man from his village smuggled his way into the prison and narrated what had happened since he left. There had been a war between the villages, which left many people dead and with many casualties on both sides. People waited hopefully for his return but with no sign from anywhere, this man set out in search for him. The two men therefore planned and escaped from the prison.

Jude ran first to his house and to his greatest surprise the main door was locked and there was no sound of life anywhere. Termites had eaten half of the main door and weeds were growing all over the compound. Then he looked and saw a letter on the ground that bore his wife's handwriting. He read in between the lines and discovered that she must have thought of him as dead though she made no effort to find out. What devastated him most was that a picture of a man was attached to the letter with the explanation that she had lost all hope in his return and out of frustration married another man. Just after a year! To make matters worse, this man came from the opposition village. The strength to fight for his village left Jude. He felt like a wounded lion, a tiger tethered to a tree surrounded by many enemies. So he left his village and vowed never to marry again.

Jude was a rich man at that time. He built houses in many towns and leased them out. Chike had tried several times to help him forget the past and start his life anew, but it was not easy. Jude failed to realize that no one has another's life in his keeping. You cannot afford to hang your future on someone else's shoulders. It was hard for Jude especially as he came from a cultural background where the family was regarded as the highest of values. I felt sad and wished I could do something to help him.

That night I wrote three letters, which I posted after one week. One was to my parents explaining where I was and what I was doing. I also apologized for not communicating all that while. I wrote to Jude and then to John. I was confident that even if the letter to John fell into the wrong hands, neither they nor John would be able locate my whereabouts.

I took my work seriously. One day I was in the forest collecting palm fronds as usual but I soon felt that I was not alone. I started singing to wade off my fear. Then I heard a whistle behind me. I turned sharply and saw a young man standing as if he was born to stand in that position.

"Why are you scared?" he asked in a carefree way.

Then he continued, "I have been seeing you every Saturday collecting these palm fronds. Normal people do not pick such dirty things here. Come let me give you work and I will pay you a fair wage. I want to help you."

He ended in a tone like a command instead of asking. As he was talking, I recognized him as one of the apprentices in the mechanic's workshop near our school.

"Help me to do what?" I retorted.

"Get a better job for you" came straight the reply.

"You know you are pleasant and hardworking" he concluded.

To be honest I did not trust him, so I continued with what I was doing. He stood there for a long time watching me. Then he said, "You do not believe I can help you? I have helped many girls. You have a better chance to do the work because you live alone. Besides, you are nice" he laughed to himself.

Since I was afraid that anything could happen to me there without people knowing, I quickly gathered the fronds I had collected and hurried away. He followed at a distance talking but I paid no heed. Later on, I had a feeling that if I continued to go to that forest alone, I might one day run into problems. But why should problems show themselves wherever I wanted to help myself? I questioned within myself.

Those brooms fetched me a lot of money for my fees but with a young man like that watching me, I feared he might be a member of a gang. I remembered the gang of boys I met when I was with Madame Patty. I decided that I would learn how to bake as fast as possible so that I can start baking all by myself. I put more interest in learning how to prepare doh-doh and chin-chin since the students loved to buy it. The woman who was my teacher was indeed a kind mother. Sometimes she allowed me to take some of the baked items home for myself.

Life in the school was difficult so I had to learn to stay with pupils much younger than myself. In addition to my school activities, I used to go to Mr. Jones for extra lessons after school and from there I went straight to the bakery. He was a patient man and a good teacher but very strict. He

43

would get very annoyed if I failed to finish my assignments. I found most of his assignments difficult to do, but I always tried to scribble something on the paper. Surprisingly, he always acknowledged my efforts and encouraged me to try harder. God blessed me with good health and strength. I hardly got sick except on a few occasions when I had malaria.

The next year I passed into Primary Two. I did Primary Two for three months and I was promoted to Primary Three. That was because Mr. Jones found me hardworking and capable of succeeding. It was not all that difficult as I had read the textbooks and did the exercises with my teacher. I did well in Primary Three and continued till I came to Primary Six after five years. In Primary Six I was still taller than most of the pupils and they thought I was the oldest in class. That made me feel lonely and out of place.

There was a lad called Uche who became a real thorn in my flesh. He used to jeer at me whenever my eyes met with his or when I was asked a question in class. He always made me shiver and out of fear I would fail a question I knew very well. He gave me a nickname, which my classmates found rather amusing.

During the third term we were asked to bring our Baptism Cards in order to fill the form for the Common Entrance Examination. Uche was anxious to see my Baptism Card. By chance I saw his and discovered that he was actually a year older than myself. I shouted to the hearing of the whole class 'old man.' Uche looked round and I kept quiet. When he turned away I shouted again. 'old man.' He tended to laugh as usual but I pointed at him.

"Uche, an old man, you are older and shorter than myself."

I was excited that I had the opportunity to take my revenge on him. The class roared with laughter,

"Ah! Short engine boy."

Within a short time he lost his temper and threw blows at me. My escape was little short of a miracle. He would have caught my eyes if I had not ducked and took to my heels. Luckily, the teacher was not in class. He left me alone after that incident. Some of the boys blamed him for what he had done.

"Why could he not take jokes as he gave to others?" was the recurring question in the minds of my classmates. We however, reconciled later on and became friends.

A group of boys and girls decided to be studying together in preparation for the Common Entrance Examination. They discussed a lot about different schools and the best in terms of their school uniform, whether the school was in town, famous and well equipped. When Uche learnt that I was doing my preparation all by myself, he offered to help me. He came from a well-to-do family. He had all he needed and more but I did not want to depend on him. I discouraged every move of his to help me. It was not usual for people to help you without looking forward to some reward in return and more so to try to change you into their own idea. That could keep you in debt all your life. I believed in the saying that every one has the capacity to change one's situation in life in so far as one has captured one's original will to change. If you say yes, your destiny would become your master. Your destiny comes from your thoughts, though some people could genuinely help you but they are few. The saying that 'one does not allow a particular stick to pierce one's eyes twice' still holds good.

We sat for the Common Entrance Examination. Many of our classmates chose the same school. When the results were released, I went to the Post Office to collect mine. I had two letters. One was from the Education Board and the other was a letter from home. My heart went inside my stomach as I went home with the two letters. I read the one from the Education Board first and it was an admission letter. I was very happy. Then I opened the other one, which incidentally was written by Patience, my friend. It read;

"*Dear Mercy,*

I wondered whether you were still alive till I heard about you from Jude. Mercy, you better leave that education and come home to meet your parents alive. Madame Ibe has completely spoiled your name and she accused your parents for whatever happened. Your sister Nelly is no longer in school. Your brother James has been sent back home. Things are really difficult. You have never written to anyone. Why are you so silent? Write to your parents at least. Anyway I am engaged to a man from Awka village. The wedding will be in December. I hope you shall be part of it on that day. Come home please! Home is beautiful.

Your friend,
Patience."

I read this letter several times before I folded it and put it aside. Then my mind went into action,

'So they never received the letter I posted six months ago? Not even Jude got his.' Then I pictured the situation in my family. "James my only hope was back at home having made no headway in life. What must have happened?" I wondered. Nelly was out of school too because of poverty, of course. I wiped the drops of tears that had formed in my eyes. This was not the time for self-pity nor tears but time to think. If I went back home, nothing would have been achieved. My little savings would go into my feeding and I would soon be back to square one. I thought of going home to get married but that was not a priority then. I would not like to marry poverty. I would like to uplift the condition in my family, and the only weapon was education. Education, yes, I must not listen to that phrase *'come home.'*

After weeping for a while, I cheered myself up with the knowledge that my family was still alive. With the admission letter in my hands, I looked up with hope and noticed for the first time Uche sitting on the branch of the tree in front of my house watching me.

"Eh! Are you crying about your success? Your face said it all," Uche said.

"How could one cry because she passed an exam Uche?" I retorted.

"How long had you been spying on me?" I continued.

He said he collected his own letter from the Post Office and ran to show me, but found me deep in thought and did not want to stop the flow of the wisdom. We then congratulated each other.

It so happened that we were both admitted in the same school. We went on to discuss on how to locate the school and the preliminary requirements needed for a start. I decided against boarding facilities in order to save money and to have time for my petty trade. Uche was disappointed, for, his parents would not allow him to live outside campus. The school was a bit far from where I lived. I had to trek a couple of miles to go to school but that was better than not to go at all. The school was one of the best government secondary schools at the time. I was so happy at my success though Patience's information about my family made me sad. It would be difficult for anyone to understand the burning drive that ruled my decision not to go home but to go ahead with my education.

Chapter Six

I woke up earlier than usual the morning I was to begin school and stretched my arms towards the horizon as if to invite the early rays of light into my world, the world of difficult decision-making and determination. I was excited with the realisation that my hope and ambitions in life will not fail me. I relaxed the tight fibres of my being that had become rigid since I got the letter from home. I was faced with the hurdles and demands of education. Among other things, we were told to report at school with our parents or guardians for identification and admission and to come with a letter of recommendation.

It dawned on me that I could not go to the school immediately without a guardian. Even though Mr. Chike and his wife represented my parents, I still had to work extra hard to provide for my fees, books and the other things I needed. It took them two weeks to make out time to present me to the school authorities. In the bargain, I utilized those two weeks to my advantage, by buying and selling biscuits, nuts and other articles that would fetch me a little money.

The principal was annoyed that I delayed for two weeks and I had no explanations to give. The admission was almost coming to a close. I devoted more time to my books and my petty trading which kept me away from distractions and other schoolmates. To the inquisitiveness of my classmates, I had no answer. They wondered where I ran to every time school was over. It was only Uche who knew my whereabouts and he always defended me when the others described me as a proud girl who never has time for others.

One time, Uche had organised his birthday party and urged me to attend. I attended with the intention to leave earlier in order to sell some articles but Uche refused.

"Can you not spare some time for socialisation?" he asked.

I stayed back, sang and danced with my mates. When it was time to open the floor, Uche was asked to pick a partner. I saw him flash his eyes at me. I knew that I would make a mess of it, so I hid behind the other girls. He kept on looking and finally went to the microphone and the next thing I heard was

"Please, Miss Mercy, come forward and brighten the day."

If I had been near the door, I would have bolted out, but I was trapped. All eyes were on me. I stumbled from my hideout. Uche was standing at the centre waiting for me. It is not easy to dance in front of a crowd, especially if it is your first time but I managed all the same.

I made few friends. One of the girls in my class was an only child of her parents. Her mother had died two hours after she was born. She was brought up by a stepmother who wished she had died too. Her life story was a pathetic one. She told me her story because she felt comfortable with me. She loved me because she had noticed that I did not talk carelessly in class nor mixed with so many people, especially boys. I got consolation from her story.

Uche was a good friend who often confided in me and most often acted as my protector against my will. I had really wanted to remain independent of any friendly assistance. Experience had taught me an unforgetable reality and that truth stared at me each time I met a new friend. The burden of carrying on alone was heavy but I struggled on. At night, the letter from Patience would torment me till sleep overcame me. The dark night would usher in a cold whirlwind. I dreamt about many things and I could hear a voice in my dream urging me to go forward and not backward.

The school was indeed interesting. There was a lot of competition especially in the science subjects. No one had ever taken first position in Mathematics, Physics, Chemistry and Biology two times consecutively. As part of our field work, we went out on excursions which was an added advantage over the other clubs. Not all those doing the science subjects belonged to the science club. I belonged to the science club and we went out on excursions to many interesting sites like the Oil Refinery, the Soap Making Factory, the Zoo and hospital. The one place we visited that held my attention and really modelled my vocation was our visit to the general hospital. It was one of the biggest hospitals in the area. I met many sick and handicapped people. I was touched by their pains and loneliness. I equated their pains with the pains of my people at home who were not only suffering from poverty, but also from the lack of basic medical care. The only clinic we had in the neighbourhood at home was far removed from the people. I remembered vividly a young lad, Peter, who died due to snakebite because of inadequate facilities there. Another woman also died there due to tetanus infection. These brought tears to my eyes. At the general hospital we visited, we saw serious cases of HIV/AIDS patients who were abandoned by their families. Some had nobody even to feed them. They looked really emaciated. I decided that I must become a doctor to help my suffering brothers and sisters.

When I told Uche about my intention of working harder in the sciences, he laughed and turned it into a joke.

"How dare you think such things in this your small head? Don't you know that you are a woman?" he said.

"What do you mean?" I queried.

"Women do not do such jobs because they are for men only. You can be a nurse or a cleaner or any other thing in the hospital and no more. Anything beyond that is a difficult job for women," he concluded.

"Difficult job?" I retorted.

"Is it that women have no brains for it or that men are afraid the women will do it better than them?" I insisted.

He said no but that he had never really seen any female doctor and that I should better do nursing. He finished by saying that I should choose a simple career for life because I would only end up in a man's kitchen.

I could not find an answer to that insulting comment but I went on to explain that doctors study illnesses and drugs that cure. When I finished, Uche said that since women were the weaker sex, I would not make it. I was annoyed again at that statement, but I promised Uche that the future would tell who the weaker sex was.

The truth that men fail to realise is that their strength lies mainly in physical prowess but when there is something that requires determination to succeed, women hardly give up the challenge. Only my determination will prove him wrong. Other girls who were touched by what they saw in the hospital said that they would become nurses so as to give their own contribution, but unfortunately, they sharing the same opinion with Uche about the seemingly weakness of women. I did not dispute their choice but I was of a different opinion that doctors could not only be men. Back in the class, the teacher asked us to write our experiences and to give suggestions on how we, as students, could help the poor. I bet you the suggestions were indeed varied.

We had good and bad teachers in the school. Our Chemistry teacher was a genius and he inspired me very much. Our Biology teacher was a carefree man with a laissez-faire attitude. He was more interested in what was under the skirt than in the head. Girls who were not interested in studies got high marks when they visited his house. I had to make a real effort.

The teachers were not well paid. Most of them organised evening classes to make some extra money which meant an extra burden for the students. I had to attend these classes because they taught better during the evening classes than the normal class periods. The teachers had several meetings in which they planned to go on strike if the government did not look into their salary situation. They were not recognised by the government. Their salaries were not graded like their counter-parts in the government offices. They felt it was not fair. The schools were not even well equipped either. Some did not have enough classrooms and staff rooms were far from being accommodating. Some had no tables for the teachers to use and mark the scripts of the students. Some teachers even used their personal allowance to provide school materials like chalk, dusters, blackboard rulers and so on, and yet they were expected to be efficient in their output. They had presented these problems to the authorities but they were not listened to. Some of the teachers used their students as housemaids. They worked in their farms, fetched water, firewood and cracked egusi for them. Some teachers, for weeks, never appeared in school. Many of them had become businessmen and women. It was a very sad situation and this seriously affected the quality of discipline in the schools. The University lecturers were already on strike. Their own problems were more and complex. The Federal University lecturers who earned more than the others wanted to be placed on the same salary scale with other Government workers. Then the state University lecturers also wanted an increase in their own salaries to bring them to the same level with the Government workers. So the general cry was, higher salaries, more Laboratory facilities, more hostels, and better roads to be built leading to the schools.

The lecturers had no consideration for the students, especially those in their final year. Many of them had spent five to six years in the university instead of the normal four years and had not yet graduated. But the students were not left out of the problem either. They were divided in their own point of view. Some argued that the strike would effect a change and a positive response if they demonstrated in solidarity with their teachers. Others argued that it would not work. Some, however, just wanted a riot. The situation was very uncertain. Apart from the reasons of solidarity, some lazy students wanted the strike, for, it would offer them an added opportunity to be idle. When I thought about the effect the strike would have on my future, I was depressed. The strike eventually came and lasted nearly a year. I regretted for the setback but I used the time to prepare for the rainy days. Determination and ambition concealed my frustration and permissive thoughts. Before the end of the strike, I opened a Savings Account in preparation for my higher studies.

Uche went to stay with his grandmother in the village. I would have gone home but I knew my plight very well. When I came back to my room after seeing Uche off at the bus station, I felt empty. I felt that even the walls of my room were urging me to go home. It was with great difficulty that I took a cup of tea and went to bed. The next morning, I found it difficult to get up. It was as if I was pinned onto my bed. I felt weak and tired. The rays of light splashed in through the cracked windows. I decided to lie still. Suddenly, I heard an unexpected knock at the door. I half sat up on my bed. The knock came again harder than before.

"Who could it be so early in the morning?" I murmured.

Reluctantly, I opened the door and behold who was there? I could hardly believe who my eyes were seeing. For the next thirty seconds or so, Jude starred at me like a ghost. I was tongue-tied. When I regained myself, I greeted and asked immediately about my parents, brother and sister. Jude answered with a nod of the head. After what seemed like ages, he exclaimed.

"You are still alive, you have to come with me. Mercy, you are no longer illiterate. Even if you are, you must come home with me. Your parents are worried and all of them blamed me that I saw you and left you again to get lost. They have not heard from you. You have the heart of a lion but enough is enough."

All efforts to explain myself failed. Jude described me as a stubborn, ungrateful and heartless person. He marched out of the house in a real rage. He had a long discussion with Mr. Chike and the two of them planned to talk to me the next day.

I was not convinced that I should go home without completing my studies. I thought Jude would understand. He did not even wait to collect my letter for my parents. I wept the whole day. My bright future was darkened by emotional feelings and misconceptions. I wrote a long letter to my parents and sent it by registered mail the next day praying that it should not get missing. The next day Mr. Chike sent for me. He asked me why I thought that the only way to success was through education? He went further to tell me that since I had not seen my parents for the past ten years, it would be better to go home and see them before coming back to continue with my studies. I had to explain the situation in my home to him and I knew very well that I would never be allowed to come back if I set my feet in my father's compound. I felt I was the only hope and the last resort to uplift my family status. Jude's indifference to my career did not destroy the edifice of my hopes because my dream spurred me on. After a month my mother replied to my letter with just a line.

"Mercy, please come home, there is no place like home."

I was happy to hear from her and that gave me a lot of consolation.

In my final year, I faced the greatest difficulty. I worked very hard to get good results that would give me direct entry into the university. I stayed awake most of the nights studying. I was part of a study group that was very diligent and ambitious. We often converged under the mango tree in the school compound to read and discuss. Our discussions brought us closer and closer. We normally diverted into other areas of interest when we got tired of reading - our future careers, politics and friendships were the recurring topics that drained the last energy in us. Some wanted to do Business Administration, others opted for Law, Engineering and other professions.

Uche opted for Law and when I mentioned that I would study medicine so as to become a medical doctor, there was an uproar of laughter. I was discouraged beyond all reasonable doubt. To my greatest surprise Uche was very objective and told them that I was already doing better than most of them in the sciences and asked what was wrong in getting a female doctor?

Reflecting on it in the quiet of my room, I felt I could do it in spite of all the discouragement. I was shocked by my friends' frame of mind. I was not going to allow disdainful minds to toy with my future career. That was not the main headache though, but my financial situation. I worked tirelessly to scale through the secondary school since I had nobody to turn to. Moreover, the fear of meeting wrong helpers always scared me. Who would be ready to train a stranger in school without asking for something in return? It was clear to me that my future success lay in my own efforts. I thought seriously what job to engage in while attending school. I stopped short in my thoughts when I noticed two inquiring eyes looking at me through the window.

"Oh! Uche," I gasped

"Why are you spying on me."

"I have been watching you for the past 30 minutes," he answered.

"You seem to be worried and far away from this planet. Now return and share your wild thoughts with me. I knew you would be upset by the reactions of our group," he said

"Uche," I said in a rather clear voice, "I have more important things to occupy my mind with than with what I see as men's prejudice."

Then Uche cut in, "Be cautious with your words, Mercy. We were only being realistic."

"Do not be ridiculous," I said sharply and continued, "Women have high intellectual powers and soul capable of reasoning. I believe it is a flaw in men's character to look down on them. What I have to do is to study hard, get the required grades and moved ahead. The power to succeed is within me."

Uche was silent. Then I continued, "I believe strongly in my bright star. My God is awake. What I need is the will to say yes and it will be done."

"But who will sponsor you?" he asked in a more concerning tone.

"I will sort that out," I answered and then continued, "Let me gain the admission first."

The admission Forms were already out and Uche had collected two forms for both of us. We filled them and waited for the examination day. We had chosen the same university.

'You have made it' seemed to echo all around me. The breeze that tickled my hair seemed to echo congratulations as it sent me dancing. My results were good and I was admitted to read Medicine. I was thrilled with my success.

A few weeks passed, the melting earth beneath me had sent shivers of panic through my mind. I feared the unknown. Only three girls opted to do Medicine in the whole zone. Among two thousand students that wrote the examination, only one hundred and eighty students were admitted. Uche also passed. He was to do Law. We went together for registration. He decided to live in the hostel. I knew I could not live in the hostel for the rents were quite high and I could not afford it.

My guardian shared in my joy and advised me to write home and tell my parents. I wondered if anybody at home would understand what I was going through. They might think I was insane, but I knew that soon I would clear all their doubts and give them joy that knew no bounds. I met with many of my female classmates, some who passed and had no hope of going on for further studies because their parents discouraged them. One girl in particular told me that her mother did not approve of university education for girls and that she was getting married. I was sorry for her. I advised her against it but she had made up her mind. She instead laughed at my madness of going in to do Medicine. She felt that I would not be able to do it to the end.

Uche remained a good friend to me. He was the only one who knew my financial situation but he could not understand why I refused his help. I valued his honest suggestions on how I could raise money on my own. I often bought cloths and he helped me to sell to the boys whilst I sold to the girls. At times I bought books recommended for the students and made them handy for them to buy. This earned me all sorts of names, but I had enough that kept me going.

I had a problem with a student called Chizo. He was from a well-to-do family and he believed in his poor head that every girl had to fall for him. Many girls of course flocked behind him. He would treat them as he wanted, drop and pick and choose. He was absent from class most of the time and girls helped to copy his notes. I often wondered why he chose to do Medicine. When he noticed that I was not interested in his friendship, he did all in his power to attract me but failed. He even tried to use Uche to get me and that never worked either. When he could not succeed, he threatened Uche too. He became antagonistic towards me. His selfish interest became so clear that other boys in the class had to intervene.

It was one of our inter university days, when the medical students would visit their counterparts in the other campuses. Normally, a quiz would be set by the hosting campus. It was Chizo's turn to answer a question to defend our campus. The question was to give the meaning of the word 'Pellagra.' Chizo stood up and was eating his fingers. To save the face of our campus, I got up and gave the answer,

"Pellagra is dermatitis and nervous symptom associated with lack of protein."

The students cheered and held me high. Chizo felt humiliated and on the way back to campus, he picked a quarrel with me but the other students challenged him. On the contrary, those girls that moved about with him joined him to make things difficult for me. I felt sad that my fellow girls were as foolish as him. They could outclass me in fashion, yes, but academically, they were at the bottom.

The final examination was tough. Even though I trembled with anxiety, I felt an inner voice which remained fluid and alive when everything else in me seemed paralysed. Mingled with the fear of the unknown, I had that deep-seated feeling that I had been chosen for greater things. When the results came out, heaven could not contain the joy in me. Uche came to share in my joy and success. He had graduated three years earlier. My medical course took eight years and only sixteen students out of forty succeeded. We were then sent to different Teaching Hospitals for Housemanship for a year. The doctor I worked under was a very dedicated man with twenty-five years of experience. There I discovered a lot of things we did not learn in the university. It uncovered for me the interesting part of the profession. There were many other things we were taught, but seeing them in reality and doing the practice made all the difference. The doctor could read what was inside you by merely looking at you. I grew to cherish the medical profession and dedicated my whole energy into it.

After one year experience, I was proclaimed a Doctor of Medicine (MD) and came to be known as Dr. Mercy Mbah. At that time female doctors were rare and sold like hot cakes. I received many offers to work in many hospitals. I had the temptation to work and earn some money before going home, but I was also worried and eager too to see my parents. With the small amount of money left from my savings, I decided to hire a car and travel home first.

"Would they still be alive to welcome their daughter coming home with difference?" was my preoccupation. The joy of coming home was mingled with fear and anxiety. Before I left, I had a good time with Uche. He took me out for lunch together with other friends. I visited his family for the first time and said good-bye to them. My guardian also invited me for a meal and offered me a big parcel. I received many other gifts and also gave gifts to others. I was grateful to Uche, in particular, for his honest love and care. When I went to the university to thank some of my lecturers who really helped me, the students who heard that I was around also came to greet me. I was proud of myself and happy to advise them to work hard as I did, to work with the determination to succeed. It was all joy and echoes of congratulations. We exchanged addresses and promised to be in touch.

To my greatest surprise Chizo also came to congratulate me. I was very happy to reconcile with him.

Chapter Seven

Home coming was an exhilarating one. I had come to realize that I made the best decision in my life. I learnt the hard way that to fight for independence in one's life is a difficult thing but necessary. I learnt that expressing my desire and working for its full realization entailed self-sacrifice coupled with pains and loneliness. In making any change, one has to risk appearing to be the 'bad guy' and has to give up certain emotions of one's familiar life. Thus, every venture in life is a risk. It is only when one has taken a leap into the unsure realm of self-responsibility that one would be free to proceed along the higher paths of growth. The highest form of love is a total free expression of choice and not acts of conformity. The more lovingly we live our lives, the more risks we take. I had taken the risk of educating myself for years. I would now proudly go home to share this joy with my parents.

I packed all my belongings and headed for the village. It took me the whole day to reach home. Before my arrival, the news had reached home that Mercy, who had been away for a long time, was coming home for good as a young Medical Doctor. People had started coming to ask my parents when that would be. The few hospitals around had started planning how to employ me without having found out my area of specialization.

When my car arrived in front of our gate, the entrance was as I left it seventeen years ago. The car could not pass through it. The door was made out of two planks held together with local woven thread and fastened with nails at the side. Termites had eaten bits and pieces off it. Nelly ran out to see who it was. I could hardly recognize her. She was tall, beautiful but a timid girl. She stood at the gate, peeped to see who was in the car. I jumped out of the car and shouted 'Nelly.' It was then that she recognized me and ran towards me.

"Mercy is back" echoed like a drum in all corners. People started running out of their huts to see me. My parents stood there gaping at me. Tears of joy filled my eyes. My mother could not shout or move closer from where she stood. She was enthralled by my sight. Tears rolled down her checks as I ran to embrace her. we stood there for what seemed like ages, speechless and only found an explanation of our feelings in our tears. Nelly joined in the dramatic scene. My father performed his own drama. He stood where he was and then suddenly sat down, murmured something and stood up again. One could see the radiating joy mingled with the confused ignorance of what he had expected from a daughter that left home so many years ago. He was not a man of many words but of quick action. He went back into his hut. Then I saw children chasing after a chicken. Nelly then went in to cook. My brother, James, had left for his place of work just three days earlier, but my father sent somebody to call him back. I wept for joy that God kept my parents alive to rejoice with me and to share in my story.

The news of my return went round like harmattan fire in the village. I was happy and grateful that my people had not lost their natural and wonderful sense of welcoming and curiousity to know the latest happenings. People crowded our house to welcome a female doctor, their own daughter.

"How did you make it my child?" was the question that came from one of the elders. "Your God must be wide-awake," he said.

He then went on to narrate how he had suffered from one illness after the other and was still suffering from rheumatic pains, arthritis and headache. A litany of how his family had suffered then followed. He was so confident that I would cure all these diseases since I had learnt 'the white man's magic.'

Another woman took over from there and narrated to me how her son died. She wished I had come with my knowledge of medicines in time. Some requested to be given some medicine there and then. My long absence from home had convinced them that I really studied medicine. Their belief in what I had become was very comforting. I listened to their stories calmly and gave a few explanations here and there.

My humble home was the same except that my father had patched the leaking roof and had made a bamboo bed for Nelly. I was happy to share the bed with her.

"Mercy...Mercy are you awake?" my father called softly from the doorway. I answered and murmured a greeting to him. He hovered uncertainly near the door and made his way back to his hut. I knew he wanted to talk to me. I screwed my eyes tightly and made a silent prayer, passionately and beseechingly with every ounce of my concentration put into it. I thanked the Lord over and over again that my family was alive to share my joy. I opened the door and entered my father's hut. There was a sweetness in his face as I entered, which poverty and suffering had not completely obliterated, but all the traces of the gentle beauty of his youth had been wiped away by the ravages of grim poverty, by the years of struggle for survival. His room was spotlessly clean in spite of the dampness. The few pieces of rustic furniture gleamed brightly through Nelly's constant care. Only the bed-mat was old, unkempt and neglected. I supposed there was no money to replace it. When he spoke, his voice was feeble but quite awake.

"I knew it was not morning yet," he started, "but I wanted to talk to you before people would start calling. I thought I had lost you forever after many years of silence."

I was happy to listen to my own father and savour again the wisdom I had missed for years.

"My child," my father continued,

"Tell me the mystery of your success. What happened that made you to leave Madame Ibe? Who was your sponsor after you left her?"

63

He told me few of the lies Madame Ibe had told them before they heard about me from Jude.

I started my story from the day I stepped out of our village to stay with Madame Ibe. It was after the dream I had that I realized that there was nobody to help our family, and I was forced to depend entirely on my own, at a great risk, to accomplish a change. I refused to succumb to the ridiculous madness of Madame Ibe. It took every ounce of my will power to move from place to place to achieve my life's goal. I told him how I met Jude and started studies. It was really a long story. When I finished, my father sighed and nodded his head several times and said, "I wish you were a man."

Then I retorted, "I do not need to be a man to do that papa. God gave equal gifts to all of us. Our intelligence is like wine which you must tap before you drink it. Once it remains untapped, one can never know how sweet the wine is."

We discussed the future and I told him that things would change for the better. In fact, things were already changing.

I had received three appointment letters from three different hospitals asking me to fill a vacancy without an interview. The hospital I finally accepted to work in offered me a bungalow to live in, a vehicle and a driver. The office that would be mine had the best of modern furniture and the instruments I needed for my work. It had two high steel and iron cupboards with glass doors containing medical and reference books. There were also cabinets of rich polished rosewood, and a table made of Italian marble supported on polished chrome bases.

The office was an epitome of superior taste. It had a tranquil beauty and softness, intermingled with red and white colours. The great soaring window was sheathed in sheer bluish-grey curtains that fell like a heavy mist from the ceiling, and when they were opened, the room seemed to be part of the sky. I smiled as I sat down at the desk. The long sweep of the marble table was neat and uncluttered, just the way I liked it, bare except for the telephone, the silver pens, the yellow note pad, and the practical metal extension lamp that flooded the desk with light. There was an air-conditioner at the lower end of the wall. On the right of the office was a refrigerator filled with drinks of every sort. I marvelled at the sense of beauty and the high taste of whoever furnished the office. As I looked around, I remembered my dream as a child.

"So dreams can come true?" I murmured.

I recalled the night I had that dream which I never recounted to anyone because it was far from being true. I was deep in my own world when I heard a knock.

"Doctor, please can the patients start coming?" asked one of the female nurses.

I told her that I would call her in a minute. I was filled with new hope wearing my new professional overcoat and with a cheerful shining face. I was as bright as a brand-new penny. I moved purposefully across the rich carpet with a flush ready to begin work. There were so many sick people to attend to and ten doctors where supposed to be working in this hospital. Only three had come by that time. Others were yet to come. Some of them had opened their own private clinics in town and of course paid more attention to them.

A woman from my village was seriously sick. Her bones were afflicted by a disease and the pain in her chest was severe. She had been to the hospital for three days but had no money to go to any of the private clinics, which the doctors from the hospital were running. Many patients from the village could not even come on account of the lack of the means of transport. I had to send the hospital ambulance to bring them. I knew that from time to time I had to use the hospital vehicles for acts of charity, and even my own vehicle too. The general hospital was meant to serve the public. It was built by the government for the people. It was actually meant to help the poor who could not afford the high bills of the private clinics.

What I saw one day made me to cry. It was my off day but I came around to visit the patients all the same. A man who was supposed to have had an operation by 8.00 a.m. in the morning was groaning in pains because at about 3.00 p.m. in the afternoon the doctor had not yet come. This was a big insult to my profession. I had to damn the consequences of doing another doctor's job to save that life. There was a lot of nonchalance from the doctors and many patients died due to such indifference. Nurses were waiting for the same doctor in the wards to come and prescribe the drugs to be given to the patients. It then dawned on me what the ordinary person goes through.

The quest for more and more money is evil and dangerous as it sways off human sympathy and love. It rubs people of the real joy of being honest and duty conscious. When I was about to leave, an emergency case came and the doctor on call had not come yet back from break, though it was thirty minutes past the time. Nobody seemed to check who did what. Some of the nurses had also copied the bad example of the doctors which was evident in the way they shouted at the patients as if sickness were a crime. I also noticed that some of the ward-maids and cleaners were neglecting their duties too. You could not breathe comfortably in some wards. Hospitals are supposed to be the cleanest places in the world, which was not so in this case. People come to the hospital to be cured and not to be hurried to their graves. I also noticed that some of the nurses were not actually trained. Some had had some six months training with a private nursing sister. They had learnt a few things and believed that that was all about the profession.

We were taught that a sick person could be difficult to handle, especially when in pain, but the patient needed more love and understanding at that time. Some could be stubborn but that should never give occasion to a nurse to insult or treat the sick person anyhow. The worse thing a nurse could do was to take money from a patient before forwarding his card or file to the doctor. The medical profession is a call to serve humanity. It is not a job to earn a living by dubious means. I decided that I would meet the hospital authorities and suggest the organisation of seminars for the doctors and nurses. The administrator listened calmly and promised to do something in this regard.

The harmattan was at its peak. In the distance I could see twinkling lights burning brightly in all the huts as the village awakened. The mist had fallen and covered the quiet village, yet one could see the piecing lights of the palm wine tapers and women going about their normal routine of fetching water. My thoughts turned to my mother who would be getting ready to join that line of action too. I prayed that the routine would one day change. I thought of constructing a pipe borne water supply system, which would serve all the villagers.

I came back to the present and prepared for my work. There were many patients and I had formed the habit of attending to all the patients even if it meant putting in extra hours. I was almost tired but I kept on. A nurse came and announced that there was a woman waiting to see me, but they would not allow her. She came late and would not go away. I told them to let her in.

I was shocked and speechless to see that it was Madame Ibe. She was nervous but her voice was distinct when she spoke. I tried to say something to calm her trembling nerves. I told her to sit down while I waved the nurse away. I kept asking myself why she came. Was she sick? After what seemed like ages, she gathered herself and began to talk.

"I have come to ask for forgiveness for the way I treated you at Lagos," she stammered.

There was something in her voice that made me relax. Slowly, the quivering in her limbs began to subside as she spoke,

"I tried to destroy the great potential in you, and I tried to assassinate your character when you left. I even blamed your parents for bad upbringing. Mercy, when I think of my children and the many girls I have destroyed in that hotel, I wish I was not born. You have a very strong will that carried you through."

Then she knelt down and said, "Please forgive me for all that I did to you."

I hurried to help her up. Tears filled my eyes. I was touched and I said, "Madame, do you know that you made me what I am today?"

She looked up at me in great surprise.

"Yes, you did, for, if you had not taken me to Lagos, *I would not have had the chance to effect a change* in my life. You set the ball rolling though on a very difficult path for a child of my age. But then I had to learn to survive the risk," I told her.

She told me that she had sold the hotel to another person, for, things were not moving well at all. Her first daughter died last year due to AIDS. The other girls ran away and she herself was not too well either. She was ready to mend her ways and start a new life.

People learn the truth of life on the altar of hardship. And when that lesson is driven home, one needs a strong will to change for the better. 'Will' implies choice. It is a desire of sufficient intensity that is translated into action.

Madame Ibe could not remain in the village because of the many gossips about her children and herself. Here the saying holds good *"He who runs after a little chick must fall whilst the chick hops leisurely away."* She was indeed courageous to have come to see me.

Many people brought their children to me not just for treatment, but so that they can receive advice on the importance of hard work and determination in life. Some offered their daughters to live with me, while others wanted their sons to marry me. I received them calmly, respectfully and asked them to give me time to consider. My first priority was to make my family comfortable. Weekends made a considerable difference in my general prospect of work. I was always at home over the weekends when I was not on call. I made sure that Nelly went back to school. I discussed with my parents about my intention to build a new house. James, my brother, was doing well in his business. The building of a new house was a joint effort.

One Saturday, since I was on night call, I planned to sleep late into morning. A phone call that jarred at my ears woke me up. I did not recognize the voice immediately. The caller started narrating how he had been searching through the Telephone Directory for my number and how delighted he was to hear me after a long time. It was along the line that I recognized the voice and I shouted, "Uche, where were you calling from?"

He was calling from his office in Abuja. I explained to him how to get to my place and the best time to come. I felt connected again. Hearing Uche's voice made me happy. He was not only an exceptionally handsome young man, but his manners and attitude were very pleasant, which in many ways set him apart from the other lads at school. He exhibited liveliness and gaiety. His face was full of vivacity like that of a woman and it had great mobility and a little wit. An easy, carefree charm was second nature to him, and he was buoyant in spirit as if he accepted life for what it was and was constantly entertained by it. There was a light-hearted independence and self-confidence inherent in him. Reflecting on how he behaved when I disclosed to him that I wanted to become a medical doctor, his first reaction amusingly portrayed his ignorance of what women can do, but when he eventually understood it, his unquenchable spirit was full of joy.

Musing over the past, I remembered the day Uche was sick in school. He refused to take a prescription from anybody till I was sent for. When I came in, he turned and said, "Doctor, o ya, cure your patient."

69

I was only in my second year in the university at that time. Following his simplicity and sense of humour, I suggested some drugs after listening to his complaint. Indeed, they helped to relieve the pain. It was only a first aid measure. After two weeks, the illness came back in full force and he was admitted in the hospital. When I came to see him, he raised his head and said, "Thanks for curing me for two weeks."

We both laughed. I looked forward to seeing Uche again to share our stories and fun. I tried to sleep again but my eyes went dry. I got up and looked through the window. The colourful birds were enjoying the beautiful air as they soared about like a jumbo jet in the sky. They were migratory birds that move from one country to another praising their maker.

The sun had risen, dispelling the moody morning, spreading its rays deep into the calmness of the moment. It would be a bright day. I could still hear the chirps of birds. As a child, I used to interpret the different sounds of birds. It was a superstitious belief that the hissing or jeering expressive of disapproval or derision in the songs of the birds was a bad omen. It might mean the death of an important personality, a man of title or a sign of a big calamity that would befall the village. If it was a joyous sound, it portrayed a good harvest or a festival. There were many other such superstitious beliefs like not whistling at night, not sweeping at night, not calling and answering your name without knowing who the caller was and many others. I do not really know how all these came about but that was part of the folklore.

A knock at the door brought me back to the present. I did not recognize the visitor but I welcomed him, offered him a seat. He cleared his throat and said that it was my graciousness that brought him to my house. He went on to explain who he was, his job and all that he could comfortably say about himself. While he was talking, I had time to observe him. He was about six feet three inches tall, but he appeared to be so much bigger in stature because of the largeness of his frame. He had a broad back and powerful shoulders. He was brown in appearance and well built, with no excess flesh on him. He had long legs and a surprisingly narrow and well-defined waist below an expansive chest. His nose was straight and fairly narrow, although it broadened slightly at the tip and his nostrils were of a flared shape.

He finished in a confused tone, not saying actually why he came and what he wanted. I thanked him for his courtesy visit. We chattered away about other matters - politics, business and people. I noticed that he was more inclined to business. He was a man from my village. His parents were friendly with my parents. When he left, I decided it was time to leave for the village.

I was distracted with the packing when I heard another knock at the door. Uche stood there looking majestic. He must have been near the village when he phoned. He was cheerful and something of his light and genial good humour seemed to mysteriously transfer itself to me. We had hardly sat down before Uche bombarded me with thousands of questions. He wanted to know everything that had happened since I left school. He recounted his own experiences and achievements. His visit brought back a lot of memories. Musing over the past, I remembered how Uche and I became friends. Then I called him "the old man" and we burst into laughter. I told Uche that I was about to visit my parents before he came. He was delighted to go with me.

A great change had taken place in my parents' home. The building was nearly completed. My father was the supervisor. He worked closely with the architect who designed the house. They were at the site when we arrived. We went round the building. Each room was self-contained and had a balcony. The engineer handling the work was a well-experienced man.

Before Uche left, I introduced him to my parents as an old friend. Then Uche called me aside and said,

"Mercy, I really came to solidify that old friendship. You know I love you and my parents had been asking about you. I love your independence and firmness of spirit as a woman. I love your will power and I felt I could tread life's path with a person of such a free frame of mind. Then coming down here and seeing your work and what you were doing has intensified that burning desire to be with you. Will you accept me as your own?"

For a brief moment our eyes met and locked and neither of us seemed able to look away. I was taken a little bit aback. I laughed and repeated the phrase 'the old man.' He kept calm and seemed to go into reflection. The calmness was contagious. I turned towards the house without a word.

"Before you go Mercy," he said, "I want to say openly and honestly that I would like to get married to you. Think about our living together forever. I am not in a hurry because I know it is coming to you as a surprise."

I kept quiet. Then I told him that I had not even offered him kola and according to our tradition he could not go away without breaking any kola. He laughed and followed me to our old parlour. My mother served us with garden eggs and some groundnut paste she had prepared. I seized the opportunity to tell my mother how helpful Uche had been to me in school. But Uche rather told my mother that I refused any help from him, that I was too strong a character. We chattered and laughed over many other things. When he left, I reflected without getting an answer to his proposal.

"Do I really want to live with Uche all my life?" I asked myself.

"Do I want to settle down in a home?"

I went into a deep analysis of what he said, "I am not in a hurry."

When I went back to my house the next day, I saw a letter lying on my table. It was Uche's handwriting. He encouraged me to take time and think about what he had said and give an answer at my own convenience. He promised to visit me again the following month and wished me well. He must have written that letter in the car and dropped it before he left for Abuja.

Chapter Eight

I soon became aware and proud of my attractiveness. I dressed in navy blue jeans and a black T-shirt with white stripes round the sleeves. My blond hair was tied in a careless knot that fell on my back. I enjoyed my work especially when the other doctors came to inquire or clarify their doubts on the right drug to prescribe for an illness. I often consulted my books to avoid mistakes. Other doctors had books to consult too but most often they had no time to read because of too many commitments here and there.

One day, I was taken aback by Patience's visit. Patience and I grew up together before I left for Lagos. My heart was full of joy as I got up to welcome her. She looked troubled. This showed itself on her face with a clear suggestion of suppressed emotions. Her figure was slimmer than I had known. I invited her to the reception corner of the office. We sat together on one cushion. I was eager to hear her story. Patience had married a shoe repairer in a nearby village and the union was blessed with three boys and two girls. Shoe- mending was not a very lucrative job. Life was hard. The children were distributed to different relatives. As she told her story, her eyes were filled with tears. I could not look at her in the face without pangs of pity. Her husband had become a drunkard and very often used her like a pestle for pounding yams. She was not feeling well but what burdened her most was her last daughter who was always sick. She had bought a drug from a chemist without any diagnose. I wrote a note and sent her and the child to the laboratory for tests. After I had prescribed the drugs for the child, I advised her to take plenty of vegetables since her haemoglobin was low. She also needed some money to buy the drugs prescribed which I readily gave her. Then she asked me how I became a doctor? I explained that it was the reward of a very strong desire and the determination to revisit the old childhood myth.

"What was this old childhood myth?" she asked.

"That if you are born poor, you must remain poor no matter how you struggle, and that if your ancestors were poor, it becomes hereditary" I answered.

"Yes I heard that," she recollected, "but I did not make any effort anyway. I was not ambitious for higher things."

Then I came in again, "The ladder is there for climbing. It is for whoever wants to risk the fall."

Then I promised to visit her the following weekend.

When I came, Patience was sitting by the fireside staring into space and her mind weighed down by problems. The light fell across the child lying at her feet on a torn mat covered with a thick old torn blanket. She looked up as I came in. She gave a quick happy shout and stood up to greet me. Patience looked paler than I saw her a week ago. Her hair, normally so beautifully groomed was unplaited and she looked dishevelled. I noticed that her eyes were red and swollen. She went out, got a drink for me and came back, put the fanta on the table and with a sigh said, "The price of being a mother often leaves me utterly exhausted. I am inclined to regret why I ever got married. Maybe I should have become a nun."

She looked at me and we laughed.

"But nuns are not those who find married life difficult" I retorted.

"I know Mercy, but I am really up to my neck. We have five children and only one attended school. The others are in people's houses as maids or learning a trade. My husband is a good-for-nothing drunkard" she went on.

There was a sharp knock at the door and it was flung open with a certain abruptness. Patience was not astonished to see the stone-faced and aggressive gaze of her husband. The smile on her face went cold and she was frozen on her chair. He was surprised to see a new strange face. He greeted me and left the room. I called him back and introduced myself.

"Oh Doctor, you are most welcome," he muttered.

Then he came back to the room, sat down and we started to chat.

"Yes I have heard about you," he mumbled, "It is a great thing for a woman to do what men can do. Yes, a woman who is valiant. A valiant soldier of a woman who can feed her family, take care of her husband."

"But you need to educate your children, educate them to be like me," I said.

Then he came in forcefully, "Oh! My children have the same intelligence as their mother - all good-for-nothing children. If I had money, I would have started with their mother. Education is good but I had made a big mistake."

He then went on to tell me how his father did not send him to school but sent his junior brother who ended up being a trader. He was able to educate his own children because he married an educated woman. He ended up in a monologue.

Patience looked at him sharply, filled with hatred and bitterness. Silence prevailed for a while. He got up and considered the conversation over. He inclined his head and left the room. Something made him pause and he looked at Patience frowning and said, "I hope you will find some food for doctor before she leaves."

Then to me he said, "Doctor, I hope to see you again some other time" and left the house.

I asked Patience what happened to her face. She was beaten by the husband the previous night. I was sad that the initial love at their wedding had faded away and had been replaced by hatred. I tried to encourage Patience not to despair. I suggested that her husband needed a job to steady his life once more. I told her to ask him to come and see me to discuss what he could possibly do. When I left their house, I reflected on many families that were in the same situation.

No education, no work, many mouths to feed and many other problems. To plan for the future was difficult for many people because there were no means.

In my village, there was great optimism, prosperity and peace as the villagers celebrated their annual new yam festival. It was a time when the in-laws and friends celebrated together. It was also the time when those in the towns came back home to see their relations. The village square was filled with happy smiling faces. My father had earlier sent for me for an important discussion. The new festival was celebrated during the dry season. I was particularly happy that I would see my brother James. I was welcomed with pounded yams and well prepared bitter-leaf soup. It was like during the good old days. We sat in the moon light outside the house remembering old stories. My father was happy and gay. He told us the story of how he knew our mother.

It was during a dancing competition between the five villages that make up Agbo town. My mother was the leader of her group. She was plumpy and full of energy. She danced so beautifully that she earned for herself the name 'atumma' (beautiful tree). Many wealthy men then came to ask for her hand in marriage but she was never generous with her smile except when she was at the forefront of the dance. In those days people had great respect for virgins. Men hunted to marry them like bees hunting for nectar. Virginity was the pride of a woman and that of her husband. One of their tactics to drive men away was never to offer their smile anyhow. One day, my mother was returning from the stream and met a group of men coming back from the farm. My father was in the group. She overheard them talking about her. One said, "This proud girl needs to be tamed a bit."

Another one asked "Why?"

"She is too stingy with her smile and hardly talks to people," the man said.

Then another said, "She is very respectful but she will not give her smile freely except when she is dancing."

Then my father came in, "Leave her alone, I like her that way."

My mother then turned and smiled at my father. And they clapped and hailed him. My father said that that smile changed his life and he felt within him that their spirits must have been connected. He then later on went to my mother's compound and met her on the way. My mother greeted him as if she had never seen him before. My mother behaved like that because a girl had to pretend that she was not interested until she was sure that her parents would accept the man. He was afraid that her parents would refuse him. Then we all laughed. My father said that he prayed in a manner which he has never done before. To his joy, my mother's parents welcomed him. They knew his own parents so it was easier for them to accept him.

After this story telling, my father asked to talk to me. James and Nelly went to bed. I sat down facing my parents. My father cleared his throat and began, "My child, your mother and I have called for you to perform our duty as your parents. The house is finished and we are grateful. We are comfortable. Our comfort will be complete if you do one important thing that remains. There is a saying that the *"a fruit like the castor oil falls on its own when it is ready. It is only those who run fast enough that can pick it where it is lying."*

Then he paused and continued after a couple of minutes, "Since you came back many important families have come, bringing wine in order to clean our mouths so as to be allowed to come in. It has not been easy to know among the lizards which one has any stomach upset since all lie on their belly. We have tried to look at their family backgrounds and history to see if they are of a healthy race, people who have never caused any trouble in the village."

He then went on to tell me about one particular family in our village whose son, Emmanuel, has been very generous to everybody in the village. My mother gave a litany of what Emmanuel's family had given to her and my father personally. He said that Emmanuel actually came to them two weeks ago to ask for my hand in marriage. I remembered his visit to my house vividly but I pretended that I have never seen him. My father told me what he was doing. He had plenty of money and often travelled abroad. My mother knew the family well. They had much land and a large extended family. After listening very intently, I inquired what answer they gave to him. My father cleared his throat and kept quiet, picked his snuff bottle, tapped it on the cork a couple of times, opened it and put some in his palm before he looked up and spoke, "Things have changed. Parents no longer have the upper hand in choosing a husband for their daughters. Experience has taught its lessons. Yet there is no gainsaying that she who deliberated first about cooking must have had more cooking utensils. This proverb does not really apply again due to western knowledge and European education. We told him to come back in three months time because we had not yet seen you. Moreover, you have received your own education which has given you some independence."

I thanked them for what they told me and promised to think about it. We went on to talk about other things. I suggested to them that it would be good to have a Well sunk which would help them and others since the one stream in the village was far. They were so happy with the idea and then we looked round the compound to see where it would be suitable to sink one. We then retired for the night.

Reflecting over what my parents said, I knew that the issue of marriage was a complex one. I did not explain to them what my own understanding of marriage was. I recaptured their own idea of a successful marriage: a family that had long life, land to farm, materially rich, generous and gone abroad and then I laughed. There was no mention of the happiness of the two persons involved, no consideration of the love and compatibility of the partners. They wanted a person that would feed you well and feed them too. That was how the culture presented it. Culture, of course, hardly takes into consideration the other side of the coin. Once a man said that he loved you and had money, you just had to accept. Many girls were living in bondage in the midst of plenty. If a man came in and gave your parents food and money, he could go anywhere he wanted with their daughter. Tradition remained oppressive as long as girls were not allowed to make their own choice in life. Some parents even refused their daughters from marrying if the man did not bring enough wealth to show off. I knew that with my education, I was well placed to effect a change. What I needed was real love and care not just any type of man; a man who understands what human dignity is all about, - "equal respect for all" - one who knows that duties are shared and that one partner complements the other.

I would like to marry a helpmate and not a master, a husband who would be a friend and would allow me to be one to him. I had to find a way to talk to my parents about all these things. My father forgot that he was very poor when he married my mother and yet they have lived happily all these years. The things they enumerated as the good qualities of a husband were the very things that help to break marriages easily. When the wealth you married is no longer there, the marriage loses its meaning. The man will indulge in all kinds of things to maintain his wealthy position in the society. Pride will not allow him to accept that things are no longer the same.

The wife, because she has been comparing herself with other women, will pick unnecessary quarrels with her husband. Then one fault would lead to another gradually leading to disaster. Then I thought about Patience, my friend, who abandoned her education halfway and got married. I was sure she did not understand what it was all about when she went into it. Marriage is a life commitment, therefore the two parties involved need instruction on the ups and downs of it. They should be prepared to face that. There is no bed of roses anywhere but the awareness is very important.

In between my thoughts, the phone rang and before I reached to pick it up, it stopped. I went into the kitchen and it started ringing again. It was Uche calling from Abuja.

Chapter Nine

There was a case of elopement in the hospital. A girl was brought to the hospital on the eve of her traditional wedding. She had feigned high fever and stomach upset. She was put on drips and in the middle of the night, she removed everything and ran off with her boyfriend. They had planned it as the only way to prevent a forced marriage on the girl.

The story is that this young man had come to the parents of this girl to ask for her hand in marriage, but since he had no money, the parents refused. They instead arranged with a man who lost his wife two years ago to marry her simply because the man had money. The parents praised the man for remarrying after a long time - two full years after the death of his wife. The girl had no love for the man but her parents insisted on the tradition of the land. This man who was already in his sixties had five children with his late wife and his first daughter was already married.

That escape brought a lot of confusion in the hospital. That old man threatened to sue the hospital if it did not produce his daughter. Nobody knew her whereabouts. My father was quite upset when he heard the story and came to find out if I was alright.

"Papa," I began, "Do you know that most parents are the cause of their children's problems?"

He looked at me sharply and asked, "What do you mean?"

Then I took my chance to explain to him my mind, "You see papa, marriage is not just a contract. It is a strong commitment in which you commit your whole life to the person you love and trust. Such a commitment lasts when there is love and trust. Even if the two persons have nothing, they can still manage. Many of the marriages that endure are those that started materially poor but rich in love. The partners built together and enriched themselves in understanding. You must always consider the interest of the two people involved and not what they give to others. Do you know, papa, that many couples look admirable outside but inside the home they live like cats and dogs?

When the initial deception fades away, the reality comes to play its havoc. When the wealth that brought them together is no longer there, things fall apart. You know, there was no way that girl could be happy in a home she did not want to belong to. That would have been a forced marriage and that is why she escaped. Papa, when you married my mother you had nothing. It was only your goodness and her graciousness that brought the two of you together and has continued up till today."

My father cut in and inquired how the story would end. I told him that we had no hand in that escape because the parents of the girl know about the young man their daughter ran away with. They did not caution the hospital to guard their daughter against a possible kidnap. Thus, the hospital has nothing to say but if I were the girl's parents, I will allow the girl to make her choice freely. There are many cases of such arranged marriages and after that nobody cares to find out how the two people are living until when problems arise, and only then people start talking. My father sighed and said, "Things have changed and changed a lot."

Then he went on to tell me how in their own time a girl will not have the courage to do such a thing – feign illness and then run away. Then I also said, "At that time the girls were very timid and brought up to believe that they had no right to decide on their future, that their opinion never counted."

My father took time to explain that women have their own powers especially the first daughters in a family. He did agree with me that when it came to some important decisions, they were simply ignored. My father left for home the next day.

One week after, I was reading a newspaper when Uche came in. I started talking with him as if he just came in from the next room, "The worst thing to happen to any person is to have little or no education, to leave school without any good qualification. The problems faced by these dropouts are many. This morning the government announced a radical plan to provide free education for everyone. How far do you think they will carry out this plan?" I asked.

"It is still paper work," Uche answered, "Let us wait and see," he added.

I imagined how the country would look like when people with little or no education were allowed to manage its affairs. Already, there were many uneducated people in many areas of public life, for example, those in charge of law and order. They have legalised bribery and dare you not comply. Two weeks before, a man had been shot dead by a policeman simply because he refused to give the requested bribe on a highway, and up till date, those responsible in the country have said nothing. This can only happen in a country where human rights and freedoms are not respected, and where material goods are more valued than human life. A pity indeed!

Then I told Uche in a nutshell what happened in the hospital and then went on, "If that girl had not had the courage to run away, she would have married a man who was forty year older than her. Why should girls be subjected to obey a culture that can destroy their happiness? Many of these things are due to ignorance. Ignorance is a disease to be avoided. Can you imagine, Uche, the protagonist of such laws being the president of this country in the near future?"

We both had a good laugh over this.

Then Uche in his usual way cut in sharply, "But this has happened in history. Some people can reason very well even without any formal education. Or are you questioning that our grandfathers who never saw the four walls of a classroom did not govern this country well at that time?"

I answered immediately, "They did but not without many mistakes. And one of those mistakes was to treat women like objects instead of human beings."

Uche actually came to get my reply to his request. I did inquire about his background, their village and how people behaved there, which would also interest my parents. We arranged that we should go home to see my parents together. Uche's parents had no problem. They had actually been praying that I should accept their son. I told Uche about Emmanuel and all that he had done to my parents, how he visited me, and the hope of my parents about him. We planned in detail how to meet my family and then agreed that he should bring his parents along.

Reflecting over the issue of marriage with Uche, I saw in him a man who was objective and free. He knew himself and what he wanted in life. He was a respectable person from my experience of him in school. He was comfortable with my freedom. This was clearly seen when I told him that I did not need his help in my education. I had expected him to have called off the friendship but he kept on. I loved him really because he saw me as his equal and a true friend. He was not threatened by my profession as a doctor.

I went home two days before Uche and his parents arrived to present their request to my parents. I had told my parents that Uche and his family would come but I did not disclose why they were coming. They came in two cars. Uche came with some of his friends. My parents did not know the family but felt that I must have known about the arrangement. My father recognized Uche but waited with eager longing for his daughter's choice. The food was prepared and served to everyone as the custom specified. Uche's father got up to speak. He gave a long detailed account of how he met me and narrated stories which I was sure Uche told him. He presented the things they brought and ended up by saying that he came to seek their consent in friendship through the union of *our son and your daughter.*

There were ten crates of beer, twenty gallons of palm wine, assorted hot drinks, six bags of rice, kola nuts, three heads of tobacco and two pieces of cloth. I wondered why they brought all these things because according to the tradition, they were required to bring only a bottle of hot drink since it was their first 'knock' at the door.

My father had also invited his brothers and the elders of the village who were around. My father then allowed his elder brother to give a response. My uncle told them that since it was their first visit, they should allow them to concert and find out from their daughter if she wanted to live in *'the place.'* They were asked to go and come back after two weeks as stipulated by the tradition.

What interested Uche's parents most about me was the fact that all the time I was in school, I had never come home with their son. For them it was a sign that I came from a well-cultured family.

When I went back to the hospital, I was told that someone had brought a letter for me. It was from my University asking me to come for an award. I knew I did well in my final year examination but I did not know that I was among the best in our department. I planned to go and to seize the opportunity to see where Uche worked in Abuja and so I phoned and informed him. He offered to come and pick me, but I told him that I would meet him in his office.

Going back to my alma mater was exciting. I met many of my friends and classmates now in various walks of life. We shared our experiences since we left school. The university had improved its structures - there were more hostels and a new library building was under construction, but there was still a lot to be done. The structures and furniture in the old buildings were not well maintained. The worst news in the air was that the government was threatening to take over the administration of the universities, to control its personnel and finances. I wondered who must have put such an idea into its head. I thought that would be the worst thing for it to do. That would affect the quality and dignity of the institutions. Objectivity that would give way to tribalism, nepotism and favouritism. The lecturers had planned to go on strike if that ever happened.

We all assembled in the auditorium before the vice chancellor and the lecturers filed in. There was an air of joy and smiles on all faces. The vice chancellor addressed us as his colleagues and there were cheers and clapping of hands. He made a very beautiful speech and thanked us for raising the quality of the institution with our good performance and conduct. After the conferring of the degrees, we were asked to go to the café where we were entertained. Many of our classmates who were not invited also came to cheer us up and to meet their lost friends too. It was after the speech that I looked around and to my surprise, Uche was sitting just behind me.

"I came to surprise you and to share your joy," he said.

I was happy and a little bit guilty that I did not invite him to the ceremony. I had thought it was not necessary, though he took it with a pinch of salt. We travelled together in his car to Abuja but I insisted that I must travel alone back to the village the next day. This was a week before Uche and his family would come to hear my family's reply about their request.

The day was windy and dry. The dry season was just at the corner. It was the month of November, the month in which I was born. People say it is the best month of the year because there is no rain and the dry weather is still mild. My parents had moved into their new home and the old thatched house was demolished to create more space in the compound. James came home for that great packing exercise because it brought a new phase in our family, a great move from poverty to wealth. James had intended to go to his in-laws with my parents and I was happy that he could manage on his own. Marriage was a very highly valued in our culture.

Any man who reached thirty years and was not married was regarded as wayward. He was not allowed to give his opinion at the gathering of his mates who were married. If the person had no means to get married, his kinsmen always helped him out.

The day Uche and his people were to come finally came. There seemed to be some mischief in the air. I had seen two men early that morning who came and talked with my father and my uncle in a rather low and worried tone. Anyway, the cooking was going on which was the sign that the visitors were being expected. Many people had been invited too. My parents had asked my opinion and I had given them my consent.

I was just about ending my morning prayer when my father called me. He told me that the two men who had come that morning were sent by the family of Emmanuel to ask if any chance would be given to them to officially make their request. The story was that Emmanuel's parents had heard that I was getting married and so sent for their son immediately. He was sad that my parents had failed to convince me to marry him. My father did not know what answer to give to them. He did not want to hurt the family because they had been very generous to them and to many others in the village. But the point is that you cannot marry someone out of pity or because he is generous.

I asked my father to send a message and invite Emmanuel to see me in person for a chat the next day. My father was hesitant but I convinced him that it was the best thing to do. I wanted to talk to him and get the real truth about his love.

The visitors came as planned. Uche dressed in a very simple traditional attire and was actually looking younger than his age. When the bride price and all other arrangements were concluded, then followed the celebration. People ate and drank and discussed. Many who were not invited also came because they knew there would be plenty to eat and to drink.

One man drank till he missed his way and someone had to help him through the gate.

The traditional marriage was fixed for a week's time and the wedding in Church was fixed to take place a month after that, actually two days after Christmas. The traditional marriage would be in my father's compound while the wedding in Church would be in Abuja. Uche was mad with happiness. He kept on looking at me without saying a word. I knew that the opportunity would come when we would share our thoughts in a much more intimate manner. His mother was happy that she would have a doctor as a daughter-in-law and she expressed that to me. My father expressed his joy to the in-laws and thanked them. He also prayed for their safe journey back to Abuja. James,also planned to have his traditional marriage two days after mine. I was grateful to God that we had made it. There is always a handsome reward for a hard working person though it may take time to come. It was a bit late before the visitors left.

The next day Emmanuel came to see me. He was looking sad but he was courageous and wore a command of authority in his approach. I took him to the inner parlour where we could talk privately. After I had thanked and appreciated what he had done to my parents, I led him onto the topic that brought us together. With all due respect to his person, I asked his opinion about marriage and marriage to me in particular. He was not ready for such a question.

When he started, it was difficult for him to speak in English. I gently told him that I loved to hear him speak in our vernacular. He told me that at first it was his parents' idea that he should marry someone with a big job and a good education like me, which would not only benefit him but them as well. Then when he visited me and found out that I was not pompous and proud like most educated girls he had met, he decided to give it a try. He was happy that I welcomed him well despite his poor ability in communication. He had been afraid to talk about marriage on

90

the day he visited me. It was not himself who actually lavished the gifts on my parents but his own parents. He had a great doubt that I would accept him because of my level of education. He was also afraid that I might insult him for not being educated.

I thanked him for his honesty and promised to be his friend. However, I tried to explain to him my view concerning marriage, that my understanding of marriage was one of mutual love between two persons who value each other in spite of what they are; people who were ready to treat each other with equal respect irrespective of qualifications or material wealth. The two must be ready to respect the freedom of each other truly and patiently. Then I told him that if he were to marry me just because I am a doctor, then he may surely fail to love and appreciate the person that I was. And if he felt threatened by one's position, then he could not live peacefully, with that person because that would condition how he saw the person. I went further to tell him that I could still help his family as a doctor when in need, so they should not feel that they were lost.

Then he said that it was true that his parents initiated the first move but he really would have loved to marry me and that if I accepted, he would pay and refund all that the other family had done.

It was then that I told him frankly that Uche and I had been good friends since our school days. We had lived as friends for long before he ever introduced the idea of marriage. When we finished, he wished me well in my decision and promised to be in contact as a friend. I begged him to endeavour to be at my wedding. He was a real gentleman. I loved the way he listened to what I said and understood that we could not actually make it together. I promised to pray for him to get a good girl that would really love him. His family did not find it easy to accept the truth when Emmanuel told them how we settled the matter. His mother said that she would meet my mother to hear what she had to say. I felt like visiting his parents just to explain to them, but I knew his mother would not be happy, and so I left it at that.

Chapter Ten

The twenty-seventh day of December was my wedding day. The birds sang unlike ever before. As I looked through the window, it was like the whole world was awake and waiting for the great church bell to announce the wedding of Uche and Mercy. The ceremony took place at ten o'clock in the morning. I was dressed in a white gown made of lace at the top to cover my shoulders. It was not a flowing gown. It had short sleeves and ended at the knees. I had a nicely decorated pink cap with a veil to cover my face. I was the epitome of beauty. Uche and his family were already waiting at the church door. He was dressed in black trousers and white shirt. Over the shirt was a black coat to match with the trousers. He looked smart in his well-polished black shoes. As I stepped out of the car, the church bell ushered me and Uche into the Church. I could hear the choir singing. It was a great day for me.

I was surprised to hear the priest tell my life story in his homily. I had never told my real story to anyone except to my parents. He told the story not just to praise me, but to let the young people in the Church realize that their destiny was in their hands and not in the hands of their parents. The days were over when children sat and expected their parents to do everything for them. Uche and I were advised to always put the other person first in our lives. Respect, commitment, love and faithfulness were the key points in his homily. Many of our classmates attended the wedding.

That was one of the happiest days in my life. Indeed, a day to remember as long as I lived. At the back of the wedding brochure, a poem entitled

"The children are not your own" was printed. It ran thus:

The Children Are Not Your Own

Your children are not your children.
They are the sons and daughters of life longing for itself.
They come through you but not from you,
And though they are with you, yet they belong not to you.

You may give them your love but not your thoughts,
For they have their own thoughts.
You may house their bodies but not their souls,
For their souls dwell in the house of tomorrow, which you
cannot visit,
Not even in your dreams.

You may strive to be like them, but seek not to make them like
you.
For life goes not backward nor tarries with yesterday.
You are the bows from which your children as living arrows are
sent forth.

Before the end of Mass, Uche and I together with our witnesses went to sign the Marriage Register. That was the first time I wrote my name without appending my father's name to it but Uche's fathers' name: 'Mrs. Mercy Adamu.' I smiled to myself. It was amazing how one could move from her home where she was born to start life anew in a new home and in a different envelopment.

After the nuptial Mass, we took many photographs to mark this great day before proceeding to the hall for the reception. The hall was full and I could hear the Master of Ceremonies calling the bride and groom to come in. Music was on. The bridesmaids were all dressed in a colourful style. We marched in to take our seats. There were speeches, the cutting of the cake, presentation of gifts and dancing. We received a lot of gifts. People ate, drank and were happy. Then we were asked to say how we felt.

Uche thanked me for accepting him as a husband, thanked my parents and his parents for their great support and love. He also thanked the crowd that came to honour our invitation. I thanked Uche for accepting me as his wife. Before I could say anything further, Uche held me and kissed me. The guests cheered, clapped and laughed. That began the new phase in my life.

Glossary

Introduction
apathy — unsympathetic
pessimistic — negative thought, lack of hope for the better
optimistically — confidently, expecting the best.
Debased — poor quality, lower in value

Chapter One
oddity — odd, unusual situation
placid — calm, untroubled
jostled — knocked roughly
nosing — inquisitive
insomnia — sleeplessness
nauseating — disgusting, unhappy
molestation — intentional annoyance
enthralled — fascinated, captivated,
perturbed — worried, disturbed
degenerated — passed into a worse physical state than which is considered normal
cart off — carry off, carry away

Chapter Two
colossus — a statue of great size
spinsters — women who remain single after the usual age for marrying.
awed — respect combined with fear and reverence
disciplinarian — person who maintains discipline
taboo — something which religion or custom regards as forbidden
hostess — woman who welcomes and entertains guests
acquainted — get used to, familiar with
comply — act in accordance with somebody's wishes, to do as requested
demarcated — mark or fix the limits of

eavesdropped	listened secretly to a private conversation
ironical	direct opposite of one's thoughts
to fornicate	to have sexual intercourse between two unmarried person; (noun is fornication)
dehumanising	take away human qualities from somebody
brutality	animal like behaviour, savagery
predicament	difficult or unpleasant situation especially one in which somebody is uncertain
heart in my mouth	be badly frightened
rag	untidily dressed person
slanderous	false statement intended to damage one's reputation
fantasy	imagination especially when completely unrelated to reality
fastidious	hard to please, quick to find fault, easily disgusted
farthing	one-quarter of a penny
harlot	prostitute, a person who offers herself/himself for sexual intercourse for money
debilitating	weakening, useless

Chapter Three

circumspection	caution, prudence
drudge	person who must work hard and long at unpleasant tasks
fate	destiny, what is destined to happen
reprimanded	rebuked
dawdle	waste time
rhetorically	have a dramatic effect and not seek an answer
tranquillity	calmness, quietness
plaintive	sad, sorrowful
fortuitous	something that happened by chance
reticence	reservedness, not revealing one's thoughts or feelings easily

| aloof | unconcerned, showed no friendship towards somebody |
| allude | refer to, mention |

Chapter Four

a pinch of salt	think that something Is not likely to be true, not wholly believe something
tortured	cause severe suffering to
blatant	very obvious, unashamed
exuberant	exciting
prodigy	wonderful, amazing
meander	wander aimlessly
tongue-tied	silent, unable to speak through fear
harassing	troubling, worrying
rotund	round and plump
ostentatious	showing off
game	animals or birds hunted for sport and food
stupefied	amazed, overcome with astonishment

Chapter Five

prismatic	clear and varied, rainbow-like
consensus	agreement in opinion
smuggled	to do something secretly and illegally
devastated	shocked
weapon	solution; the way out

Chapter Six

rigid	stiff; unbending
inquisitiveness	inquiring into other people's affairs
bolted out	run away quickly
modelled	take something as an example for one's action
genius	exceptionally great mental or creative ability

laissez-faire	carefree attitude
abortive	coming to nothing, unsuccessful
misconception	misunderstanding
prejudice	opinion, like or dislike
ridiculous	deserving to be laughed at, absurd
dignity	true worth, the quality that earns or deserves respect
insane	mad
antagonistic	showing a feeling of active hostility or opposition
housemanship	practical experience with an experienced doctor in a hospital

Chapter Seven

conformity	in accordance with something, obeying something
harmattan fire	moved very fast
rheumatic	painful disease with stiffness and inflammation of the muscles and joints
arthritis	inflammation of a joint or joints of the body
screwed	closed
obliterated	removed
dissipated	dispersed
succumb	to yield to
epitome	summary of, a perfect example of
nonchalant	carefree, uninterested
dubious	dishonest
assassinate	destroy
vivacity	high spirited, lively
buoyant	cheerful
rancour	ill-will, spite
migratory birds	birds that go from one place to another with the seasons especially to spend the winter in a warmer place

flared	gradual widening at the bottom
voracious	greedy

Chapter Eight

myth	story, handed down from olden times
hereditary	passed on from parent to child or from one generation to following generations
dishevelled	untidy, ruffled
valiant	brave, determined
monologue	a long speech in a conversation, which prevents the other people from talking
compatibility	ability to exist together with
bondage	slavery
helpmate	companion

Chapter Nine

feigned	pretended
havoc	widespread damage; destruction
protagonist	leader, advocate of a cause
tribalism	favouring ones tribe against other tribes
nepotism	giving of special favour to ones relatives
auditorium	part of a theatre, a concert hall, in which an audience sits
way-ward	not easily guided, childishly headstrong
mischief	playing tricks
pompous	feeling or showing that one is much more important than other people

Questions

Chapter One

1. Describe the extent of poverty in the family of Mr. Mbah.
2. What are the main thoughts that made Mr. Mbah to send Mercy to Lagos?
3. Describe the characters of Mr. and Mrs. Mbah.
4. What made Mercy to look hopeful to the future?

Chapter Two

1. Narrate Mercy's experience in Lagos.
2. Why did Mercy leave Madame Ibe for the first time?
3. Describe the life and the character of Madame Ibe.
4. How does Madame Ibe view the dignity of human life?
5. Why did Mr. Shilar refuse to help Mercy?

Chapter Three

1. How did Mercy leave Madame Ibe for good?
2. Compare and contrast Madame Ibe's character and that of Mrs. Patty.
3. Describe Mercy's life in her second home.
4. How did Mercy discover that Mrs. Patty did not want her progress?
5. List the superstitious believes in the Novel.
6. "How could I penetrate that soft place in her? " Discuss this in relation to the story in this chapter.
7. Compare and contrast the life in Lagos and in Mrs. Patty's house.

Chapter Four

1. Why was Mercy sad after reading the letter from home?
2. Discuss for or against the rules in Mrs. Patty's house.
3. How did Mercy cope with those rules and restrictions?
4. Narrate how Mercy left her second home.

Chapter Five

1. Name and explain the different jobs Mercy did to educate herself.
2. Why did Mercy refuse any help from those boys who offered to help?
3. Why did Jude decide not to re-marry?
4. What was Mercy's idea about a bright future?
5. Describe Uche's character.

Chapter Six

1. Describe the teachers' situation in the schools.
2. Why did the teachers go on strike?
3. Write about those teachers who exploited the students?
4. What were the difficulties Mercy faced in her final year?
5. Describe the character of Chizo and his friends?
6. What sparked off the enmity between Chizo and Mercy?
7. What part did Mr. Chike play in Mercy's life and education?
8. Describe Mercy's character at Uche's birthday party?

Chapter Seven

1. Narrate how Mercy was received back in her home after many years of absence?

2. Why did Mr. Mbah make the statement "I wish you were a man"?
3. How did Mercy's dream come true?
4. Describe the situation of things in the Hospital.
5. List the points that portrayed Uche as a good friend to Mercy.

Chapter Eight

1. Explain the situation of things in Patience's house.
2. Explain the meaning of "The childhood myth"
3. Describe Mercy's feelings on her visit to Patience house.
4. What were Mercy's parents' ideas about marriage?
5. Narrate how Mercy choose her vocation to do medicine?
6. What were the influences of education on tradition?

Chapter Nine

1. Why did Uche visit Mercy at her work place?
2. What is your idea about forced marriage?
3. Describe Emmanuel's character.
4. Explain the traditional marriage of Uche and Mercy?

Chapter Ten

1. Describe the wedding of Uche and Dr. Mercy.
2. Mercy stands as an epitome of an admirable character. Discuss.